# Bruce!

David

**JEREMY P. TARCHER/PUTNAM**

a member of

Penguin Putnam Inc.

NEW YORK

# Bruce!

## Adventures in the Skin Trade and Other Essays

## Bruce Vilanch

Most Tarcher/Putnam books are available at special quantity discounts for bulk purchases for sales promotions, premiums, fund-raising, and educational needs. Special books or book excerpts also can be created to fit specific needs. For details, write Putnam Special Markets, 375 Hudson Street, New York, NY 10014.

**JEREMY P. TARCHER/PUTNAM**
a member of
Penguin Putnam Inc.
375 Hudson Street
New York, NY 10014
www.penguinputnam.com

Library of Congress Cataloging-in-Publication Data

Vilanch, Bruce.
Bruce! : adventures in the skin trade and other essays / Bruce Vilanch.
p.   cm.
ISBN 1-58542-046-8
1. American wit and humor.   2. Performing arts—United States—Humor.
I. Title.
PN6162.V55          2000                    00-032577
814'.6—dc21

Printed in the United States of America

1   3   5   7   9   10   8   6   4   2

This book is printed on acid-free paper. ∞

Book design by Gretchen Achilles.
Interior photos © Ron Krisel

## acknowledgments

This all began when Jeff Yarborough, then-editor of *The Advocate,* thought it might be fun to let me wail publicly once a month. His successor, Judy Wieder, persisted in this wayward mind-set, which has been facilitated immaculately throughout by Anne Stockwell. Dan Strone at William Morris had the fiendish idea to turn it all into a book, and David Groff made it his last project before abandoning Tarcher/Putnam for cyberspace. The home team—brace yourself, there are several of them—kept me going through the years it took to create, collect, and cull: Michael Wolf, Jackie Scissors, Craig Austin, Pete Shilaimon, Jim Chambers, Bart Drumm, Rob Thomas, Theo Sjolberg, Kai Hand, Adam Sher, Brad Cafarelli, Rick Heineman, Rob Shuter, Stan Coleman, David Miercourt, and the production squad at *Hollywood Squares,* especially John Moffitt, Pat Tourk Lee, Steve Radosh, Susan Abramson, Andy Friendly, Sean Perry, Jay Redack, Naomi Grossman, Dave Feranchak, and Rebecca Lee. Of course, everything I do and have done has been guided for at least thirty years by my manager and close personal goddess Joan Hyler (this is amazing, as we are both only thirty-two). And I would be more than remiss if I didn't thank the people who have allowed me to be a collaborator in their personae, most especially Billy Crystal, Whoopi Goldberg, Robin Williams, Nathan Lane, and the woman who wrote my act, Bette Midler.

## To Henne Vilanch

superstar

and, oh yes, my mother

# contents

# Bruce!

# introduction

Here's what being on TV every night does for you: People mistake you for a cousin who disappeared in the '60s, or a member of the Grateful Dead (which could be the same thing), or either Ben or Jerry or somebody who is in some way associated with food, or someone they met at a dinner party six months ago whose name they can't quite place, or a serial killer, or *Smackdown* wrestler, or the guy who sold them some really bad stuff at a concert, or Crazy Hymie who wants to sell you a stereo so desperately he will scream until he bursts a vein and is carted off to intensive care, or their ex-brother-in-law who still owes them money, or somebody else who's on TV every night, usually a consumer reporter who spends his days crashing through doors of liposuction clinics to expose something heinous.

You also get to write a book. And hopefully, nobody mistakes it for anybody else's.

I called the book *Adventures in the Skin Trade* for a couple of reasons. First of all, it sounds dirty, and that seems to attract a lot of readers. It certainly attracts me. Even though, looking at the jacket photo, I am clearly not my type. But I am one sexy beast, just ask—well, their names are all in the book. Maybe yours is, too. LOL. That's cyberspeak for "laugh out loud," for those of you still in the twentieth century. I know, I didn't want to hook up either, but after succumbing to cable, call waiting, and condoms, it seemed little to ask to enter the new millennium.

The other reason I chose that title is that getting under someone's skin is pretty much what I do. Not in the Ralph Nader–pesky gadfly way. But I write the words a lot of other people say. And in order to do that, I have to make a fairly thorough study of how they speak, how they move, what they think, and what they need to accomplish when they open their mouths. Sometimes, in the quiet of my lonely room, I have to Become Them. Not for long—I don't have a Mae West gown hanging in the closet like the characters in *Dirty Blonde*. But there is one hanging in my head just in case. It's like a second skin, but it really can't even be that, as I could never get it over my first skin.

The observations you are about to experience are not *all* about that. I've stepped out a bit in the last few years and become Mein Own Performer, and I've tried to share some of what has happened to me since becoming the poster boy for late-blooming icons. It is an ongoing Carnival Cruise and I'm happy to be your social director, if only for a while.

Many of these essays were written for *The Advocate,* which is delighted to be known as the *New York Times* of Gay America. That means many of these essays have a gay perspective—but then so do I lately, as I have come to realize that one of the several minorities of which I'm a member (male, Jewish, homeowner) has decided to shed its thin protective coating and become visible. I've been out for so long that I only recently realized that you apparently have to make a public declaration of it, like when you get a passport and you swear you won't overthrow any governments. So I guess this book is it, if every other appearance I've made hasn't qualified.

One more thing—I recommend a bathrobe and some Chinese food while reading. That way if you find something you really don't like, you can cover it with a soy stain so you will never be troubled by it again. This will not work if you're on a plane, unless of course you're flying to China, and in that case, don't you have some stolen secret formulas you should be reading?

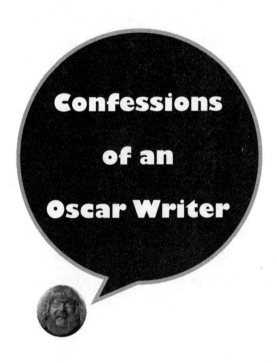

# Confessions of an Oscar Writer

There is a small, devoted cadre of people who don't believe the Academy Awards show is written.

I've met them. At none of the better houses, but they are out there. They believe everyone on the Oscars is spontaneously witty. Or stupefying dull. Whatever.

*"It's pretty much up to them, isn't it? I mean, nobody writes that stuff . . . Someone does?"*

I once served on a blue-ribbon panel of TV writers, none of whom I had ever heard of, judging the Emmy entries in the variety-writing category. After the first hopeful—an award show—was screened, a hand went up.

"What was the writing on that show?" a blue-ribbon panelist inquired. The winner that year was a stand-up comic's concert act..

So this isn't a condition confined exclusively to civilians (people outside of show business—"nonpros," *Variety* calls them).

People who actually make a living in the factory of illusion believe their fellow professionals step out onstage ready to greet the largest single audience of their careers with no script.

The fact is that everything you hear on Monday's Oscarcast has been written, rewritten, re-rewritten, fretted over, spelled out phonetically, garbled in a fax, left in a tuxedo jacket, cleared by an expensive legal team, delivered by bonded couriers with scripts handcuffed to their arms, smeared with aloe vera, chewed by the Abyssinian kitten, dropped in the pool, laughed at by valet parkers, obliterated by canasta scores, shredded during a shrill custody battle outside Gymboree, and inadvertently tucked under the bottom of the Norwegian blue's cage.

Part of this, of course, is because the Oscars is like the Super Bowl.

People who never watch a football game dutifully drop

what they're doing at least once a year to take in that big match. People who never go to the movies and people who never watch television (except maybe to watch football) tune in to the Academy Awards.

If you're going to play in the Super Bowl, it's better to be on the winning team. So you'd better train.

For actors who normally spend nine hours a day in a comfy Winnebago on a cell phone and another twenty minutes in front of a camera, the idea of performing live in front of a real audience is fiercely daunting. Especially when they have no character to play.

Most acts never have had to establish a stage persona. They don't know who they are onstage when they're not playing somebody else. A few gifted actors—like Billy Crystal, Whoopi Goldberg, Bette Midler—are also solo performers, so they know who they are when they're alone onstage. Shirley MacLaine not only knows who she is; she knows who she was.

But most of them have always depended on the character the writer has given them to play.

And Oscar Night is no exception.

The writers have to come up with something for them to play. Sometimes it's the dread Banter. The writers always try to avoid that, but frequently it's what the actors actually want. ("It'll humanize him," one icy hunk's publicist insisted to me one year. Trust me, Adolph's Meat Tenderizer couldn't have humanized this guy.)

More often than not, you go with informational stuff about the category. This gives the actor a reason to be there (other than his own fabulousness), plus it shuts up the whiny nerd at your party who always asks, "But what is Sound Effects Editing?" (This is also usually the guy who wins the pool because he guessed the tender Flemish picture about the leprous carp fisherman would win Best Foreign Language Film.)

Now that the writers have figured out what the actor should say about Sound Effects Editing (who can hear over that category, anyway?), the material must go to the actor, the actor's agent, manager, publicist, holistic pet psychiatrist, feng shui master, ex-wife who always had good taste and the mealy-mouthed little assistant who has a degree in CompLit from Pepperdine and never has read anything quite so puerile.

They fax their notes.

"She doesn't want to be funny" is the note I've gotten from every single actress except Lucille Ball, whose great-grandchildren will live elegantly on what she made from never telling a writer she didn't want to be funny. After the material has been hashed and rehashed, the actor himself arrives for rehearsal and a little more hash-slinging.

And then it's time for the show. And the meticulously polished material is performed, frequently with the following pearls of ad lib:

**a)** "I told them that wouldn't work."

**b)** "Could you move that card up, please?"

**c)** "Gosh, I can't see a thing without my glasses."

**d)** "I'm absolutely falling out of this dress."

**e)** "Hello, Jack."

And the Oscar goes to: "Don't blame me. I didn't write it."

# America's Favorite Fruit

"It's ours to screw up."

I said this to Whoopi Goldberg as we did the Private Ryan crouch-run to our respective boxes on the first day of taping of the new *Hollywood Squares*. She smiled at me. I think. Her head was bowed so as not to crush her do. The squares themselves are 5 feet 2 inches high, so unless you're of the munchkin persuasion, everything is done either sitting down or in a profound hunch. *Hollywood Squares* first showed up on America's radar more than thirty years ago. The first version, both morning and evening, lasted fourteen years. A second attempt, in the '80s, ran three. The Third Reich began in September, and so far, so good. From the beginning, *Hollywood Squares* has been a very gay place.

Wally Cox, the petite bespectacled comedian (his hit sitcom was called *Mr. Peepers*) and onetime roommate of Marlon Brando, was the earliest detectable presence. The original center square lumbered out of the other end of the spectrum—Ernest Borgnine. But soon the show found the waspish Broadway sidekick Paul Lynde, and he became the squares' literal centerpiece. (Q: "On April 14, 1912, Seaman Frederick Fleet spotted . . . what?" A: "His favorite chinos.")

From then on it was "Tillie, bar the door." Such out (or outwardly) types as Charles Nelson Reilly, Billy DeWolfe, Rip Taylor, Jim J. Bullock, Wayland Flowers and Madame, Dom DeLuise, Richard Simmons, and Jimmy Coco all found a comfortable home in one or another of the squares. Innuendo and double entendre established a permanent address at *Hollywood Squares,* and celebrities who played the gay card got the biggest—and easiest—laughs. Well, say "big" and "easy," and you get two things: New Orleans and me. When the new production team approached me to be the head writer of the current revival, what did you expect me to say? "I'm terribly sorry, but I'm busy doing a monograph on the use of the subjunctive by Nicolai Gogol." I couldn't wait. Of course, they said the show was going to be different, more upscale. I had visions of Royal Shakespeare Company week: "I'll take the Redgrave sisters to block."

But once we started prepping, I knew that some elements of the squares were chiseled in pink neon. When Whoopi came on board to be the center square, she noticed it too. So she suggested to King World, the coproducers, that they might want to go a whole new way with a host—me. Anxious not to offend their new star, they tested me, just like the old days at Metro. I went in with a whole bunch of sparkly-toothed, besuited glamour boys and pretended to host the show. I figured I might be a tad much for mainstream America. But two things happened: First, Tom Bergeron burst out of the pack and established himself as the best-possible guy for the job. Hip, clever, cute, fast—everything you want in a date. Second, the King World pashas called and said, "You know that you're not exactly what we're looking for in a host. But we'd love to have your energy in a square." They'd been watching their old tapes, and they'd been paying attention. That doesn't happen a lot in TV. So I assumed my place in the great lavender lineup. And heavy is the mantle that was placed upon my delicate, birdlike shoulders. Because unlike anyone I can think of on *Hollywood Squares,* I was well known for being gay long before I was well known.

Early on, when asked the question "You are the most popular fruit in the United States. What are you?" I replied, "Humble." It got a huge laugh—and from an audience that is largely recruited from the Farmers Market next door to the studio. Nevertheless, I steeled myself for the memo. None ever came. In fact, I've never received a note to pull back or go easy or re-think or any of the euphemisms producers use in an effort to keep a show in the middle of the road.

Backstage we go through periodic fits of worrying that the show is too gay—also too old, too young, too black, too white, too Jewish, too Monica, too Newt, too tutu (but only when a ballerina or a bishop is on). But the people who write the checks don't seem to be worrying. So you shouldn't either.

By the way, the correct answer is "banana." Talk about gay.

# Ready for Our Close-Up

I never had to call her Miss Ross. "I've been meaning to speak to you about that," she said when I mentioned it the last time I saw her. We were on a plane, and I was busy introducing her to people she'd never met, including Stephen Schwartz, the song-writer whose "Corner of the Sky," from *Pippin,* she had recorded back when she was going through her Motown Does Broadway phase. "Ooh, that was a good one," she said, cooing to him, and then proceeded to sing it, a cappella, word for word.

"I can't believe she remembered that!" he said to me.

"I can't believe she's flying commercial," I replied.

I have known and worked with our cover girl, who told me to call her Diana shortly after I met her, since the early '70s, when I found myself unknowingly becoming a part of gay pop history. I was a journalist in Chicago in those days, but every now and again I would get cast, usually as a sight gag, in a movie or TV show filming locally. Oy, have I got a reel.

One day a casting director called and asked me if I could play a couple of scenes as the flamboyant-as-I-wanna-be dress designer in the new Diana Ross vehicle called *Mahogany*. The script had originally been written for Liza Minnelli (probably under the title *Knotty Pine*) and was being refashioned for Miss Ross.

As I'm sure everyone reading this knows, *Mahogany* is about a struggling dress designer who goes to Europe with a gay high-fashion photographer, becomes the toast of the modeling world, becomes the dress designer she always wanted to be, and then chucks it all to rebuild the ghetto with the firebrand politician she loves. *Sigh.*

My part was the designer who first hires her as his apprentice. The director was England's eminent Oscar-winner Tony (Vanessa Redgrave's former husband, who died of AIDS complications in 1991) Richardson.

Tony had two things going against him, aside from the fact that the script was miles beneath him. He was working under the assumption he was making a Tony Richardson picture when what he really was making was a Diana Ross picture. And Diana couldn't understand a thing he said. He spoke in a picturesque, singsong, heavy cricket-team dialect, and she would frequently look at him with a puzzled expression, too polite to ask him to repeat himself. She was, of course, hot off *Lady Sings the Blues,* and her mentor, Berry Gordy, decided that, as she never had a problem understanding what he was saying, he should direct the picture.

So Tony went home, and Berry took over and declared that the story had to move the hell out of Chicago and over to Rome as quickly as possible, Rome being a much better venue for the endless hours of fashion shows and outdoor modeling sessions he intended to shoot.

So instead of hiring her, I refused to hire her. Mahogany, that is. I had to rewrite the scene on the spot. In fact, Diana and I did it together. Then, because everyone was in a big-ass hurry to get to Rome, I wrote the dialogue in large letters on a piece of wrapping paper that sat on a table in front of me. Diana stood so we could both read the dialogue and play the scene.

This was Berry's first day at the helm, and he was so anxious to get started, he was ready to shoot the rehearsal. He ran around, authoritatively hollering, "Lights! Camera! Action!" Diana pointed out that her hair was in curlers. "Hairdresser for Miss Ross!" he bellowed. She gave him a little peck on the cheek and disappeared into her trailer for two hours.

By the time she emerged, I had learned the lines, but I had not learned how to sew, which is what Berry had me doing during the scene. In the first take I sewed the scarf I was wearing to the coat Diana was wearing. When she turned to leave, she wrenched me off my stool and began dragging 250 pounds of dress designer behind her. In our next take Billy Dee Williams (whom we called Dark Gable) opened a door, and the lines flew off the table and into the camera lens. On the third take we got it right, which was good because we had already blown Berry's hoped-for reputation as a first-take director.

The picture went on to be one of the Gay 101 movies, and years later, when I met RuPaul, the first thing he said to me was, "I loved you in *Mahogany.*" This is how I know he's a genius.

# Rockin' Robin

Walking through San Francisco with Robin Williams is like walking through Sherwood Forest with Robin Hood. He owns the place. Every tree, every rock, every nook and cranny hides a cohort waiting to leap out and cry, "Robin, let's":

(choose one from this list of offerings made during a casual stroll) "take a picture,"

"make a picture,"

"do a doob,"

"play Jumanji,"

"give me a dollar,"

"go visit my mom,"

"play with Gershwin"
(probably the chow puppy at his feet, but could be code
for something else),

"record a video,"

"nanu-nanu,"

"get some pesto,"

"some latte,"

"some crystal meth"
(they still like their drugs in San Francisco—they still *love*
their food)

"buy a loft"

"hang out with Francis"
(probably Coppola, but could be code for something else)

"sign my stomach"
(definitely not code for anything else)

"say something to your fans in Fukouka"
(tempting, but then the camcorder jammed).


The cops we meet (one Asian, one Anglo), the street kids,
the boys in wigs, the girls in leather, even the tourist-weary San
Franciscans trying to live a real life in this last metropolitan
Utopia—they all view Robin as one of their own. And why not?

"He lives here, dude!" one of the nouveau hippie/homeless says proudly to the uncomprehending Japanese camcorder hound who stalks Robin down Haight Street. "Leave him alone!"

Like his bandit namesake, Robin left the pleasures of the palace for the fertile fields of home. Unlike Robin H, he doesn't steal from the rich—he takes their money and makes them richer. His name has been above the title of at least eight movies that grossed more than $100 million in their initial North American release. Two of them, *Jumanji* (in which his love interest is Bonnie Hunt) and *The Birdcage* (in which his love interest is Nathan Lane) passed the centenary mark over the same weekend, meaning the malls of the world were filled with people laughing along with Robin.

And Robin has made out pretty well from this. As an associate remarked when Robin wasn't Oscar-nominated for his drag triumph in *Mrs. Doubtfire,* "He'll just take his $25 million and go home." Maybe, but like Robin Hood, he can't stop giving to the poor, not only through the semiannual Comic Relief telethons he cofounded and cohosts, but also with the dozens of local benefits he has spearheaded, not to mention the movie production he has helped steer San Francisco's way. "Robin Williams, could you spare a quarter?" another long-haired Kurt Cobain clone asks as he swirls by. Robin's hand goes in his pocket as he turns to the kid, who looks stunned. "No, no, I don't want your money, man. I just wanna shake your hand." Like Robin of Locksley, Robin of SF is a touchingly easy touch.

Unlike his namesake, Robin Williams's band of merry men are all inside his head. They pop out with no warning, usually accompanied by a change of voice, an explosion of arms, and a cautionary "Don't be afraid!" What everyone used to think was drug-induced behavior ("Cocaine? You should see me on caffeine") turns out to be Robin's standard way of expressing himself. He takes ordinary conversation as far as he can stand it and then bursts into a character riff to better explain his feelings, like those people in musical comedy who have to sing and dance because mere words can't contain their joy, or sorrow, or lust.

In general, he is a man given to bursts. Bursts of laughter, bursts of color in his clothing, bursts of physical energy. Between the bursts, things can get downright tranquil and reflective and people, even strangers who approach him on the street, can be treated with a kind of deferentiality that makes them giddy. They can't believe this celebrated millionaire genius megastar is paying such attention to them. It must be some sort of joke. But it's not. He is respectful of people and their quirks. It's the fuel that fires up all the other stuff. And when he suddenly goes to flame—another burst—everybody he's ever met and every tick they ever revealed is released into the atmosphere.

This may be one reason he lives in San Francisco, a city full of individuals, where every coffeehouse on every corner has its own line of T-shirts and refrigerator magnets. It's the last great walking city, because the weather usually cooperates, and if you avoid the hills, you may actually come out of it alive. (Fran Drescher, who has played Robin's girlfriend twice now, in *Cadillac Man* and the current, San Francisco–filmed *Jack,* tells of watching her small dog do its business on the top of a hill, praising the dog, and then racing down the hill with a pooper scooper to get to the bottom before the business did.)

Robin likes to walk around the town. It's the city where he left his heart and came back to claim it. "I came back here when I left school and lived at my parents' in Tiburon, which is this island in the bay. I worked at a place in Sausalito, the kind of place where they would advertise for a waitress job and girls would come in and they would take a Polaroid and have them fill out an application. Then they would throw away the applications and look at all the Polaroids. Maybe they hired somebody, maybe they didn't.

"There was a guy working there as a waiter and we did some kind of act. A lot of it is hazy now. I remember lots of stoned nights diving into the bay." There were many other addresses and many other kinds of acts that evolved into the manically political stand-up that attracted attention some years later. Among the addresses is the one we are standing in front of now—Beaver Street.

"I was just attracted to it somehow. Perhaps it was the name. You think? Nah!" On the most recent *Comic Relief,* the production staff had a pool as to how long it would take Robin to get to a dick joke. The show started at 6 P.M. The winning guess was 6:07. And there had been a five-minute opening number. "The dick jokes were okay, but after I did the talking vagina, even I had to say whoa, where can I go from here?"

"He's in love with his dick," one of the producers said. "Can you blame him?" Similar charges have been leveled at more than one star, but few have made their phallusmania so amusing, or shared it so willingly. Robin's penchant for royal blue ad-libbing precedes him, of course, and an appearance on a live show like the Academy Awards produces a steady stream of anxious executives tactfully reminding him of the trouble he could get them all in. "I got away with a few things this year," he reminisces in triumph, "the stuff about the Woody doll from *Toy Story* ('I had a Woody all through high school. I used to wake up with my Woody and play with it'), but then there was one line they asked me not to use. It was in the Chuck Jones tribute. He is the great Warner Brothers animator, and I wanted to say 'Working at Warner Brothers is like having sex with a porcupine. You're one prick against a thousand.' I hated losing that.

"I loved Beaver Street," Robin continues, "and it looks exactly the same." There are some differences. Beaver Street is smack in the middle of the Castro, which back then was gay, but right now is Gay, the center of all Gay life in a city where Gay is a political force of some consequence. "We had a loft and so we were above a lot of other buildings. We could see and hear everything. I learned every name you can call a man during sex. At Halloween it was insane. We'd look out the window and see thousands of wigs being teased simultaneously."

From Beaver Street it's a short walk along Castro, past the fabled old Castro Theatre (current attraction: Sal Mineo, Juliet Prowse, and Elaine Stritch in *Who Killed Teddy Bear?*, with an organ selection as prelude; Robin performed at a benefit to kick-start the theatre's restoration). A couple of blocks down is something that wasn't here when Robin was, but has become the city's newest bizarre tourist attraction—The Barbra Streisand Museum . . . known locally as Hello, Gorgeous!

"I can't believe she did it so small," Robin jokes and then feigns elaborate surprise when told the storefront shrine was put together by fans without diva authorization. It's a converted Victorian, actually (as is half of San Francisco) covered from ceiling to floor with Barbra-ana. There are several dozen Barbra mannequins ("made special for us by a guy in Oakland") dressed up in famous Barbra outfits, remainders of all the merchandising from the recent concert tour, items of a peculiar fan mentality (Barbra clocks, Barbra notepads), interactive exhibits (push the button and the Barbra mannequin moves and lip-synchs), and a glass-walled room decorated in 1962 Barbra items, including an old TV that plays her first special on a never-ending loop. For $6.50 you can have a Polaroid taken of you and the Barbra mannequin of your choice. It's the kind of eccentric enterprise that could only survive in San Francisco, a town that has supported the campy *Beach Blanket Babylon* revue for over twenty years.

"It's you!" cries a buff guy in black jeans, black eyeliner, and silver staples and rings in his ears and nose.

He is in the middle of painting one of the dozens of Barbra portraits that adorn the walls. "Be very careful," Robin intones, appraising the work. "Make the slightest mistake and it's Jennifer Grey." He casts about the room and lights on another oil with an unfortunate nose. "Look! Glenn Close after a prize-fight!"

The owner is reverential. "Do you know Her?" he asks hopefully.

"Know her? I opened for her!" Robin laughs.

"Oh, yes, of course, on the One Voice concert," the owner immediately remembers, and you fear he may take himself off in a corner and beat himself up for forgetting.

"That was a night," the opening act muses. "It was a benefit in her backyard and she had more greenery than Spain. Very hard to be funny in a setting of intense natural beauty."

They're waiting for him outside the museum. A couple of tourists and a real estate agent with a bunch of open-house signs under his arm. "Can I interest you in anything in the neighborhood, Mr. Williams?"

"Got anything on Beaver Street?"

"Yeah, I thought that might catch your eye."

Farther down Castro, a leather fetish store is having a Father's Day sale on collars and leashes. They call it Daddy's Day. "Oooooh, Daddy," Robin says, instantly morphing into one of his merry men, "buy me that smart choker with the spikes." The movie he's about to shoot is called *Father's Day,* the long-hoped-for Robin Williams/Billy Crystal vehicle in which they play divorced men tricked into raising a child they are both told is theirs. "No collars or leashes, but we are both buffing up. And we don't know why. I'm on this insane killer diet and Billy is lifting weights. The other day we looked at each other and said, Why are we doing this? I guess it's something these *guys* do. Maybe we're channeling."

After *Father's Day* comes *Flubber,* the big-budget special-effects remake of Disney's classic *The Absent-Minded Professor.* "I don't know why we're remaking it. I showed the original to my kids the other day (Zack, twelve, Zelda, six, Cody, four) and they loved it. Of course, this version will have effects like you've never seen," says the survivor of *Jumanji,* "and the flubber is actually a character. But"—and he looks deeply and seriously into the middle distance—"I don't want to spoil it for you.

"Which way to the hunchbacks?" Robin asks the smiling clerk. We are in the humongoid Disney Store in Union Square, the same Union Square where rumor has it Robin used to work as a mime. "Never! That was Robert Shields (of Shields and Yarnell) turf. He'd kill you if you stepped on it. I worked indoors. And never as a mime." It's a few days shy of the release date of *The Hunchback of Notre Dame,* and all the merchandising isn't quite in place. Nevertheless, we find a Quasimodo plush toy. Robin handles it almost with awe. "Look . . . he's got a hunch. And a slow eye. And bad teeth. I would get it for Zelda, but she hasn't seen the movie and I . . . I think she might cry." Like lightning, he turns to the clerk. "Have you got a Hunch-Back-Pack?" Giggles. "How about a Hunch-Lunch-Box?" Nope.

"Ahh, what good is the place?"

As we leave, a mother points for her child. "Look, honey, it's the genie, from *Aladdin*." The child seems confused. Then he smiles. Unbeknownst to any of us, there is a big picture of the genie right behind Robin.

The toys are much more grown-up in North Beach, the old Beatnik part of town. "Where is she? She used to be right here!" Robin is standing under the sign that used to advertise Carol Doda, the world's most famous topless act and for many years a San Francisco landmark the size of the Transamerica pyramid. Doda's old club, the Condor, is still there, but all trace of her seems to have disappeared. "Oh, my God!" Robin says, looking heavenward. "The nipples are gone!" Beg pardon? "They used to have big red nipples on Christmas and now they're gone. The humanity!" Doda herself is evidently still around.

"I played tennis with her last week," Robin's driver reveals.

"You did?" his boss answers, jaw dropping. "Wait a minute—she can play tennis? She can hold the racket? She can see below the net?"

The driver reveals little. "All I'll say is, I won."

Robin looks at him. "C'mon. It *had* to have been doubles."

Across the street from the Condor is another old haunt, the City Lights Bookstore, founded by the seminal Beat poet Lawrence Ferlinghetti and virtually unchanged since. "It's the only bookstore in the world with a Surrealism wall," Robin notes, then slides into a little dialogue with a merry man: "Where's the Existential section?" "Sometimes it's here, some-time's it's not." "Where's the section on Abuse?" "Fuck you!" "Where is the Dada section?" "I don't care."

In the old days, the drill was to buy a book and take it across the street and read it in Tosca, a bar filled with poets, stevedores, and opera queens, all presided over by Jeanette Etheridge, a chic blonde in iridescent barrettes who, when not breaking up bar fights between athletic intellectuals, helps organize the San Francisco International Film Festival. "Really, we should salute *you*," she says when Robin bumps into her at Enrico's, an Italian café on the street, "for making all these movies in San Francisco."

"I like to work at home." Robin shrugs. So he made *Mrs. Doubtfire, Nine Months,* and his most recent, *Jack,* here. "A movie takes three months. I'd rather be home than away. If they tell me they're going to film it here, they get me." Well, not exactly. Otherwise you might be seeing him Friday nights as Nash Bridges, San Francisco dick. The material has to pass a certain muster. Like *Jack,* Francis Ford Coppola's tender and funny story of a ten-year-old boy with the body of a forty-year-old man . . . "But it's not a fantasy, it's a medical thing, so it's rooted in reality. It's a sweet little picture," Robin says wistfully. "I hope it doesn't get lost behind all these big guns." That doesn't often happen to Robin's movies, and when it does, it almost seems calculated. Little pictures like *Seize the Day* and *Being Human* can't have been intended for a mass audience. But they offset behemoths like *Hook* and *Jumanji,* which clearly are. It's almost a karmic career: do something for art and you will be rewarded later with commerce. "It's not a precise science, you just never know. You can't think about it. Who knew *The Birdcage* would be this big?" Or *The Fisher King* or *Dead Poets' Society* or any of the other iffy projects Robin helped vault into the stratosphere.

The stratosphere, or at least someplace where the air is thinner, is where we are now—"The Haight!" Robin cries as he leaps out of the car. "My homeland!" We've just cruised through the Lower Haight, which is dingy and borderline and actually resembles the fabled Haight-Ashbury that hosted the Summer of Love. (If you are old enough to remember the Summer of Love, you are officially old enough not to be trusted.) A bit farther along and you come to the corner of Haight and Ashbury, the cosmic center of capitalist hippiedom. It's almost pristine. The stores shine, the cops patrol. The crowds take pictures of each other. Mostly they're tourists or bargain-hunting GenX couples, but every tenth person looks like a variation on an old Blues Project album cover. Each block sports one, but no more than one, clutch of homeless kids in Janis and Jimi jeans, sitting quietly at a storefront, panhandling demurely.

"Amazing . . . some of them are third generation. You know, it all used to be real," Robin comments as he searches for some psychedelic landmark of a previous age, "but now it's sort of like a theme park with hippie characters. Okay, today, you're the toothless one with the puppy and the bandana. You be the Grateful Dead burnout. You're the philosopher, or is it just Tourette's syndrome?"

As if on cue, the counterculture's newest pseudo-star, Manny the Hippie, appears. A baby-faced blond of twenty-two, he shot to notoriety when David Letterman put him on the tube during a week of shows he aired from San Francisco. "Robin Williams, cool!" Manny intones, attempting a handshake.

"I want to say this is swag," Robin says, referring to Manny's catchphrase from TV, "but I can't remember if that means good or bad."

Manny has a different agenda. "You know, MTV's been calling about you and me doing something together." Robin's face betrays nothing. Maybe he once was a mime after all.

Like most everyone here, Robin takes the Haight for what it now is, an atmospheric mall with acid overtones. There are running shoes to be bought at one place he knows, a book on hold at another, and a store specializing in Hawaiian shirts that seems to know him really well. But just when it seems almost suburban, a stoner without a tooth in his head walks up to him and says, a bit woozily, "I know you from TV. You're Manic, D.I.!" A simple "nanu-nanu" would have sufficed.

"Where do you suppose he *got* that?" Robin asks incredulously over dinner at Rubicon, a friendly-tony place he co-owns with Coppola, DeNiro, and about a hundred other people, "Do I *look* like Manic, D.I.?" He pores over the menu, "I love to come here. They have great fake wine."

Off everything for years, he enjoys the illusion of boozing it up. Bloody Mary mix, imitation champagne—at any moment, there's the possibility he will begin snorting the Sweet 'n Low. "You should see when Francis comes in. They serve him his own wine, from his own vineyards. He has these incredibly knowledgeable conversations with the sommelier. It's awe inspiring."

The check arrives. Or rather, doesn't. "Your money's no good here." The manager laughs. But Robin wants to make sure the waiter gets his tip. "It's already gone into his Swiss account." The manager laughs again.

"You're sure?" Robin replies with real earnestness. "I really want to be sure he gets it." It's Robin of Locksley returned, the Robin who bought a plane so it would be easier for his family to travel, who performs for free when local columnist Herb Caen has a street named after him, who has helped finance his drama schoolmate Christopher Reeve's recovery from a paralyzing accident. The downtown crowd pays little attention to him, although one boisterous table from Chicago actually asks that he come over to say hello. On the way back from the men's room, he actually does. He says something, they laugh, and he sits down. What did he say to them? "I don't know. I did thirty seconds and got off." Odds are, they'll remember.

# Sure Bette

How to be very, very popular: Walk into a gay bar in Winnipeg, Canada, with a fistful of free Bette Midler tickets. You will be experiencing the divine with lightning speed. For the past eighteen months, I've been looking for America—and the warmer parts of Canada—with Miss M and her entourage, of which I was the most conspicuous member if you don't count the

Harlette who dressed in theme clothing for each city (a peach in Atlanta, a revolting colonial in Boston).

I wrote and rewrote the show in each city—something I've been doing for Bette since slightly after the Paleozoic Era, when she first made her mark at a tar pit on the west side of Manhattan. It had been ten years since our last trek, and we didn't know what to expect. Bette had become the kind of movie star whose Winnebago was being bandied about as a possible cover story by *Architectural Digest*—I mean, the full-value, industrial-strength-diva type of stardom, which had happened at Disney, no less. (Two words we never thought we'd see in the same sentence: *Midler* and *Disney*.)

It's never *just* been Bette's beginnings at New York's baths that have attracted her gay following. It's her unwavering attitude, her example of how one can happily continue to be "us" in a world populated and ruled by "them." She does this not by being gay but by being joyous.

So we set out with our latest edition of vaudeville's last gasp and discovered that those of us who are still alive are well—even though most of the people whom a traveling star meets are invariably ill. I'm sorry, but that's just the way it is. Every dressing room is filled with flowers and requests from people who are really sick. Everybody on the local crew has somebody nearing what Miss Peggy Lee calls that "final disappointment" who needs to come backstage. In the real world all this makes sense, and you deal with it like a caring human being. But this is the surreal world.

I know huge stars who have stopped performing because they are convinced that their appeal is limited exclusively to the lame and the halt. It's one of the things that never figures into anybody's fantasy of what big-time showbiz stardom will be. But you deal with it, and in addition to inspiring you, it makes you actively seek signs of blessedly healthy life wherever you go. And as a gay man who has been everywhere and back the past year and a half, I'm telling you we're in pretty extraordinary shape. If we don't kill each other.

One of the wonderful things about Bette's gay audiences is their diversity within their gayness. When Miss M and her three circus rings pull into Dodge and set up tent in whatever hockey rink they have inherited for the night, Irving Average American gets a lovely view of the full rainbow of our community. Shockingly, so do we.

Leather queens, dykeez in Nikes, older gents with long-held degrees in Judyism—they are all there, eyeing one another from behind their popcorn. Bette makes fun of everyone with jokes that celebrate our characteristics and are distributed evenhandedly across the footlights. Of course, it helps to have a common enemy—and we do. However, he/she/it varies in each town.

Fortunately, in every town we played, there's a gay hot line, a gay switchboard, or, last resort, a gay Realtor line. After a few hours of heavy sledding, hot-line staffers were usually delighted to get a call from somebody who was wondering if there were any local homophobes Bette Midler might make fun of in front of twenty thousand people the following night.

"Girl, have you called the right place!" was the reply I got seventy out of seventy-one times, and then the tea began to boil. It was thanks to the hot lines that we got on familiar terms with such bizarre, high-concept individuals as Fred Phelps, who pickets AIDS funerals in Kansas, or Sue Myrick, a North Carolina politician who makes Jesse Helms smile, or Nathalie Pollock, who claims she was fired from a Winnipeg TV station because her breasts were too big.

In Vancouver they faxed two pages of assorted dish. In every case they were offered tickets to the show. Some took them, many donated them to AIDS charities, and one particularly serious guy in Charlotte, N.C., said, "You know, I'd love to, but frankly, I'd have to give you my name, and this is an anonymous service. I couldn't violate that rule." If you think that's high-minded, how about the guy in Minneapolis who said, "That would fall under the category of personal gain, and that's not why we volunteer for this service." For a group that is supposed to be xenophobic and self-absorbed, we seem to have a nice touch of nobility about us.

Or maybe I was just catching all of you on one of those days when Newt says we're being good citizens.

**Swell Mel**

It takes a lot to get me to a Mel Gibson picture. They all sort of pale after *Tim*. That's the one in which he plays a very young, bare-chested, marginally retarded fellow who spends most of his time striking picturesque poses on some lovely Australian beaches and the rest of his time slamming it to Piper Laurie. She's warm and wise and older, and, well—why hide it?—I have frequently pictured myself in the role. It's seen me through many a winter's evening. Nothing much Mel has done since then has reached me on quite that level. He held his own opposite Tina Turner, he isn't afraid to show his butt (or someone's stand-in butt), and he even got away with *Hamlet,* though he is the one moody Dane I've seen who truly would have benefited from tights.

I guess I'm just the sort of fan Mel Gibson is supposed to be afraid of. So it was with some alarm that I discovered I am now supposed to hate Mel, not just for some remarks he might have made in some foreign language but for a gay-bashing movie he has directed and starred in. Just when I'd gotten *Tim* down in my mind, frame by frame.

As you can imagine, I couldn't accept this burden without actually seeing the movie, a task quite a lot of people have evidently not taken upon themselves. Off I trundled to the mall in my trench coat, babushka, and sunglasses, looking like Elizabeth Taylor checking into the Betty Ford Center—if Elizabeth Taylor were blond with a beard, in which case she would be Shelley Winters. I shucked my picket-deflecting disguise, dropped one hand into my popcorn, and hunkered down for two hours and fifty-seven minutes of love, honor, and dismemberment called *Braveheart.* Turns out it's a kilt caper, not unlike the one I saw a while ago with Liam Neeson, one of the high points of which was Academy Award winner Jessica Lange squatting and peeing on a beach. This one is also an epic, set during the reign of Edward I when Scotland fought for its freedom, led by a rogue warrior named Sir William Wallace, who had a chic habit of putting on powder-blue war paint before riding into battle.

English history is full of fops, and *Braveheart* and *Rob Roy* (the Neeson picture) both have them. The fops in *Rob Roy* are heterosexual and unsurpassably evil. They rape, pillage, scheme, murder—you name it. The fops in *Braveheart* are homosexual, but they are bus-and-truck versions of the ones in *Rob Roy* and probably not nearly so monstrous as they were in real life. One of them is the notorious Edward II, and the other is his pretty-boy lover, who gets tossed out a window by Edward I in a fairly severe fit of pique. I kept waiting for the simpering, pathetic, stereotyped portrayals of homosexuals that the protesters had warned me were coming, but pretty soon things were wrapping up—all except for Mel's bowels, which were being systematically unraveled by his torturers. Then the credits were rolling, the bagpipes were playing, and a Samoan woman in a uniform was drumming her fingers against her broom waiting for me to leave the empty popcorn box on the floor so she could sweep it up. I staggered up the aisle and into *Wigstock: The Movie* next door to meditate on what I had seen.

It's impossible to ignore Hollywood's history of turning gay people into symbols of evil. But it's also impossible to ignore history. We claim Michelangelo, and we also have to claim Edward II. You can't do a movie about William Wallace without depicting his enemies. No one thinks the gayness of Edward II was the reason Mel Gibson did this movie. But it is a genuine element of the story, impossible to ignore. Because it is not absolutely central to the character played by Mel Gibson the actor, you'd think that Mel Gibson the director might play fast and loose with these villains, making them lisp, mince, roll their eyes, wear makeup. In fact, they do none of these things.

There appears to have been a conscious effort taken to have the actors *not* portray their characters in stereotypical fashion. Edward II is depicted as treacherous but not swishy. He is clearly not going to make much of a figure as king, but that's not because he's prone to sissy fits, it's because he's such an obvious snake. His lover is murdered not because his wrist is droopy but because Edward has put him in a politically dangerous position. The history is pretty clear on this, and the treatment here is—sorry to report—pretty subtle. It would be nice to jump on the bandwagon and give Mel a few whacks, but he doesn't deserve them. Not for this. Movies frequently reinforce the notion that homosexuality equals Badness or at the very least a sort of second-class citizenship that ends in violence. In *Braveheart* badness equals Badness. Nevertheless, it gets picketed.

The other night I saw Terrence McNally's new play, *Master Class,* in which Maria Callas quotes Aristotle Onassis several times on the subject of the fags who worship her, the fairies who dress her, the fags who make up her audience, and so on. Nobody was picketing. McNally, a gay playwright, reinforces a stereotype and uses derisive language to do it. He did it before, in *The Lisbon Traviata,* where an opera queen turns out to be a murderer. No pickets. McNally's a hero and can do no wrong. Mel Gibson's a pariah.

I'm trying to be a better person. I'm trying to work up a fantasy in which I'm Piper Laurie and I meet Terrence McNally on a beach. I'm open to it. I really am.

**Magic Moments**

Elizabeth Montgomery probably will not be remembered as a great actor, but she was. She *will* be remembered as a witch, which she definitely was not. It's just one of those things that history will think of her as the nose-twitching suburban haus-frau Hecuba on the series *Bewitched,* which will linger on Nick at Nite and Turner by Day and Stella by Starlight and all those other high-end cable channels that will spend next to nothing to buy it, thus ensuring it never gets broomed.

Lizzie, as I knew her for about twenty years, was the first actor to get what was happening in Hollywood. She saw that the serious women's-issue movies—the ones that would have been made at the studios in the pre-TV days with divas such as Bette Davis, Olivia de Havilland, Joan Crawford, Barbara Stanwyck, Ingrid Bergman, and so forth—were not going to be made as features anymore. As the traditional women's audience abandoned the theaters for the most part, the guys running the networks noticed that that very audience was watching a lot of TV. A versatile TV star like Lizzie could play the full range of roles once available to studio actors such as Susan Hayward and Joan Fontaine if she was willing to do them on TV. And so she did. She was the first.

For twenty years Lizzie averaged two or three TV-movie "events" a year, about the same number of movies Lana Turner averaged in her studio heyday. She played Lizzie Borden, she played Etta Place, she played an upscale urban rape victim in the graphic *A Case of Rape,* she played sleuthing crime reporter Edna Buchanan, she played a blind private eye, she played a mother who talked her kids into killing their father, she played a woman who ran away from home to be a circus clown, and she did a fair remake of *Dark Victory*—if a gay boy can say such a thing without being struck by lightning. She had the career a woman actor would kill for, only she had it on TV—and TV will remember her as a witch.

I was silently musing on this at her memorial service when her husband, Robert Foxworth, got up and read a letter he had received shortly after her death. The writer identified himself as a gay teenager. He said he had always loved Lizzie as Samantha on *Bewitched* because, as he viewed it, Samantha was just like everybody else in her small town, except she was different. Both her Darins (ask somebody who watches the show—he'll explain) loved her despite, or perhaps without regard to, her difference. She had a full life, some of which was because she was a good person or, more accurately, a good witch. The gay teen went on to say he found this portrayal personally empowering (his words) because it gave him the means with which to survive his own life.

Now, I don't know about you, but it never occurred to me that watching *Bewitched* was an empowering experience. I doubt it ever occurred to Lizzie, except that it empowered her to buy a house and a couple of horses. And, of course, to be the first woman actor to take advantage of the opportunities TV was offering in the movie area. Empowerment, of course, comes when that inspiration forces you to summon up your courage and take a position for yourself, a position that lets Them know that They can't get away with It.

I was silently musing on empowerment (been doing a lot of

silent musing lately) when the radical—and not-so-radical—queers of San Francisco took their action against Eddie Murphy. You have to admire these guys. They've been drumming their fingers since 1981, waiting to hold Eddie to account for routines he did in his first major-league HBO special. They're a very serious lot. They scared Robin Williams away from playing Harvey Milk when they took him to task for alleged gay stereotypes in his act—Robin lives, eats, and breathes San Francisco. They've been silently waiting for Eddie to land on their turf. And land he did, during David Letterman's recent sweeps-week sojourn to Rice-A-Roni-ville, where little cable cars swish halfway to the stars. Our Town. The activists were there in force, led by a gay city official, whose participation made the action very difficult for anyone to ignore. Unlike other recent protests of allegedly homophobic movies, the world has had fifteen years to digest the material in Eddie's old act. Although some of it has always been funny—the notion of Ralph Kramden beggin' Ed Norton for some nooky is hilarious—most of it is vile, bashy, clinically misinformed, sterotypical, AIDS-paranoid . . . well, all the things the protesters say it is. Everybody knows this. Including—surprise—Eddie.

In an apology issued after the protest, he characterized the material in question as the half-assed thoughts of a twenty-one-year-old man uttered at the beginning of a plague no one understood. He's thirty-five now, and he knows better, and he's sorry. I believe him. I also believed him in 1985, when, as a twenty-five-year-old man, he made a high-five-figure donation to New York's first major AIDS benefit, a show I cowrote called *The Best of the Best.* It benefited Gay Men's Health Crisis and other local AIDS charities. His name is in the program as a major donor. He's been waiting to clear that name, and I'm glad the guys in San Francisco empowered him to do so. And empowered all of us to turn him from a bad witch into a good witch. Now we can stop wrinkling our noses at him.

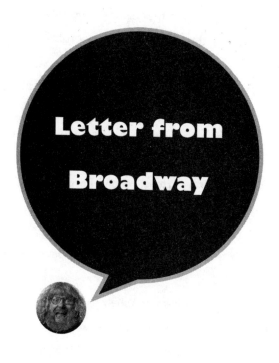

# Letter from Broadway

I guess it's safe to say Broadway has changed, especially when you're nearly trampled by a horde of blue-haired ladies who are storming their way into the Wednesday matinee of *Bring in 'da Noise, Bring in 'da Funk*. The same gals who were cheering Sammy Davis Jr. thirty years ago are now cheering the anti-Sammy, Savion Glover, who has created a show that reclaims tap dancing from the Sammys of the world. Maybe it's Glover's energy they're responding to; maybe it's his anger and intensity. It sure ain't his charm. But they eat this revolutionary up, these matrons, in a way they never would have back when Sammy reigned.

Perhaps what has happened to Broadway is that after repeated exposure to the joys and sorrows of so many minority groups, the old majority audience has finally found a place at its table for everyone. Kind of like what we are hoping the country will find. Even *Victor/Victoria,* widely viewed by the theatrical community as a crowd-pleasing clunker, has gender confusion at its core. (It also has Julie Andrews spending most of the evening in a bathrobe and pajamas, which induced yawning in my section.)

I was on the Main Stem, as *Variety* likes to call it, cowriting the Nathan Lane part of the Tony awards show. The Tony awards, for any heterosexuals who might have started reading this by accident, are presented for excellence in the Broadway theater. The network that runs the show insists that it come in at exactly two hours—nominations, awards, baffling production numbers, tearful thank-you speeches, heartfelt salutes, and all. So writing the show becomes something like packing a hard-sided suitcase. You keep tossing stuff in until you notice the bag won't close. Then you take everything out and try refolding it all, thinking that will somehow make it fit. Then panic strikes, and you begin tossing things over your shoulder in gusts until you can sit on the thing and squeeze it shut. I knew I was taking the whole evening too seriously when I found myself uttering foul curses at Uta Hagen. She wasn't reading the TelePrompTer fast enough, and we had to cut one of Nathan's bits. Life's too short to be wishing the kind of things I was wishing on old Uta. I had to get a grip. Or a stagehand, a propman—anything.

The Tonys were fun to work on this year thanks to a series of controversies that kept the media feverish with speculation—the biggest was whether or not Julie "I am sixty going on seven" Andrews would get out of her snit (she declined her nomination) and show up. She didn't, and the voters, who were predicted to show her that they were bigger than she and give her the award anyway, decided to take her at her word and gave the award to Donna Murphy for her performance in *The King and I.* Ironically, this is a role I've always longed to see Julie Andrews perform—in fact, would much rather see her perform than the one she labors through in *Victor/Victoria.* I'll take a hoopskirt over pajamas any day.

*The King and I* is still something to see, however, with its sets, which made me think for a moment that Norma Desmond had become queen of Siam, and with the radiant Donna Murphy and especially Lou Diamond Phillips. Yeah, him—the *La Bamba* guy. He plays the king kind of like the talented quarterback who has taken the lead in the high school production. He strikes a pose after nearly every line that seems to say, *How do ya like this shit? I'm the king!* It's very entertaining—and brave: If you were an actor, would *you* want to go up against a legend? I'd never seen the king played by someone so young, or who at least projects such youth, and it gave the piece new life. Of course, those crafty old pros Rodgers and Hammerstein probably never realized they had created one of the great gay subtexts in the forbidden romance of the slaves Lun Tha and Tuptim. The two exquisite ballads "I Have Dreamed" and "We Kiss in a Shadow" might as well be carved in stone at the gay Valhalla. I've never seen a production of *The King and I* without immediately relating Tuptim's plight to, sigh, my own. Some years ago B. D. Wong got up at a Los Angeles AIDS benefit/tribute to R&H and sang the two songs in a medley that shocked, then delighted, a packed house.

The night after *The King and I* was the night I saw *Rent.* Again, for any of you heteros who are still tuned in, this is the musical sensation of the season. It's a '90s version of *La Bohème* set in a loft in Alphabet City, and at first it plays like *The Mickey Mouse Club* with syringes. And it's Anything Can Happen Day. The underpinning of *Rent* is full of terrific rock songs and bravura singers, but what made me marvel is the central story, which is about three couples. One of them is lesbian, one is a man and a transvestite, and one is straight. These three couples go about their romantic business, and nary a word is said about their sexual identity. They are couples, with the problems of all couples. The audience responds to them as people, not as gay people or straight people. I don't think I've ever seen it on a

Broadway stage—I know I've never seen it on TV. *Rent* takes a Bohemian context and uses it to mainstream gay characters. I hope it runs forever. And if Broadway hasn't changed quite enough for that, at least put it in repertoire with *The King and I* to remind us of the days when the best we could hope for was a couple of numbers in the subtext.

# Camp versus Kitsch

Summer's over, but camp's still in session. You remember camp. It's the time-honored gay art form, related by gay marriage to kitsch. Actually, they're sometimes mistaken for each other. But they're really worlds apart. Kitsch is the art of bad taste. Not bad taste as in doing O.J. jokes at a benefit for a domestic-abuse clinic. Bad taste as in those tiny statues of Elvis and Ann-Margret that have little pools at their feet where you're

supposed to place votive candles. That's kitsch. All those paint-
ings of big-eyed kittens wearing berets and smocks or of
clowns sadly removing their makeup. Your relatives probably
have a houseful of these things. You may have grown up sur-
rounded by them. It's a cruel world.

Kitsch happens because straight people don't know better.
Maybe it's inherent. Maybe that's why there are so many gay
decorators. Maybe we just don't get that gene. Camp is something else again. In its purest form camp is failed seriousness.
Richard Nixon was about the highest camp our age can hope
to produce. And straighter than Dick you didn't get. Everything
he said had that hollow ring; every pronouncement, that drip-
ping upper lip. His body language, the way he stuck his arms up
over his head like Pinocchio being lifted to a higher shelf, the
perpetual five-o'clock shadow that gave him that faintly degen-
erate look—it was hilarious. He couldn't help himself. As he
got deeper and deeper into disgrace and started making "I am
not a crook" speeches, Nixon's camp quotient skyrocketed.

No matter how deliberate it may look, camp happens to
straight people by accident. Gay people, who have been made
to feel so trivial and insignificant over the centuries that they
can never take themselves too seriously, rarely stumble into it.
We do it by design, usually to take the starch out of straight
people. When straight people attempt it, they wind up with
*Mystery Science Theater 3000* or something equally lame. Oper-

ating on the "its so bad, it's good" theory, they take Japanese horror movies and put their own sound track to them. (Woody Allen, another notoriously straight person, did it in *What's Up, Tiger Lily?* and as far as I'm concerned, it didn't need to be done again.) This is low camp, collegiate and willfully ignorant of the fact that the stuff being spoofed is inane to begin with.

Occasionally, a gay person will stray over into camp. Barbara Jordan, captured in full eruption at one of the Democratic conventions, enunciating every word as if the syllables had been handed down to her at Sinai—now, there was a lapse. But when gay people go camping, it's rarely unplanned. Drag queens, with their extreme versions of what women will wear, are holding a fun-house mirror up to the straight world. They're commenting on what straight men seem to want from women and on the lengths straight women will go to to give it to them. For all their efforts, most drag queens look like comments on women instead of real women. And that's deliberate. It's performance art, the art of failed seriousness, the art of camp. At its best, camp is an elaborate, artistic way of telling the public all about the emperor's new clothes. When Terry Sweeney used to come out as Nancy Reagan on *Saturday Night Live* and dispense that first lady's cheerful poison, it put all the phoniness of the real woman's appearances into focus. When RuPaul commands the catwalk, he's showing just how manufactured and contrived the idea of supermodel really is. When John Waters makes a movie in which a perky suburban housewife can gain control of her life only by becoming a perky suburban serial killer, he's showing us how the benign American landscape has sprouted a few new weed patches.

Camp is all around us these days, both planned and spontaneous. Ted Koppel's explaining in "Elvis has left the building" tones why he felt it necessary to quit covering the political conventions is my recent favorite. Why was he there in the first place? Was he expecting genuine news? On the new and mystifying MSNBC cable channel—which seems to be a version of CNN set in a Starbucks—hunky Brian Williams (the latest Canadian to take over American TV) was attempting to show us exactly where the TWA jet went down, only it was too soon for the graphics department to scramble to the drawing board, so he was reduced to whipping out an AAA map and a pencil, pointing to a blue spot off Long Island, and saying, "Um . . . somewhere about here, I think." Top that, Jerry Seinfeld.

On almost any night you can cap your day with a full, rich dose of Tom Snyder, who has borrowed Nixon's upper lip and can be counted on to hold forth with solemnity on virtually any subject. He is never more amusing than when offering tributes to other television journalists, usually referred to as "those dedicated men and women who keep the watch that we keep," and so forth. And for Best Extended Camp Performance of the

Year, the hands-down winner is likely to be Kathie Lee Gifford, who attempted to make *herself* the victim when it was revealed that her clothing business was something of a sweatshop. If publicists are called spin doctors, then Kathie Lee is a spin neurosurgeon. She even makes House calls.

# Beneficial Benefits

My mother quit the catering business shortly after theme bar mitzvahs became the rage. First she did a Wild West bar mitzvah, which was conducted on horseback. The parents described themselves as Jew Dudes who loved everything outdoorsy. Then came the circus bar mitzvah, in which the thirteen-year-old star appeared in the center ring as clowns and exotic animals gazed on and a bevy of cooks tried to whip up kosher cotton candy. There was a Ziegfeld bar mitzvah, at which the boy of the year was discovered behind scalloped drapes riding turntable, which twirled once and deposited him on top of a curved staircase. But it was the Japanese bar mitzvah that made her toss in the towel. The specter of sumo wrestlers framing the kid's entrance while sushi chefs struggled with gefilte fish was just too much. She had to go on retreat to get in touch with her Jewish roots. I know how she felt.

I have just come home from my 435th gay/lesbian/AIDS/political/humanitarian/transgendered/joyfully empowered/fund-raising/consciousness-raising/awareness-raising/barn-raising/toe-tapping/chicken-chomping benefit this year. I am now the Elisabeth Kübler-Ross of benefits, having gone through all seven stages of the peculiar brain death that attaches itself to organizing or attending such events. Maybe I spent a tad too much time in Anger and Denial, but I have managed to limp my way into Acceptance at last.

So I have no problem with benefits anymore, not even number 435—Gay Bingo, a great favorite of little old ladies of all ages and both sexes. The beneficiary was a local AIDS service organization, and the callers were all drag queens in varying stages of disrepair. "B-12" got a lot of laughs, but nothing near the response accorded "I-69." The players, some of whom had never indulged in a pastime as blue-collar as bingo, eyed their cohorts, the hardened, fixated people who will play bingo anywhere—church or synagogue, gay or straight—with incredulity. They were eyed back with suspicion. *You don't suppose these newcomers are getting all the good cards, do you?*

The hard core regarded the drag queens with even more suspicion. *What's taking these big dames so long, and why are they making all those jokes? There's money to be won!* What a photo opportunity for Fellini. Really, he died far too soon. Paul Rudnick, another gifted social observer who thankfully is still with us, wrote about an AIDS hoedown in his play *Jeffrey.* He was exactly two steps ahead of reality.

I have now attended my second "Two-Step Toward a Cure" benefit, at which Beverly Hills matrons of all ages and both sexes pay big bucks to get up in their finest fringe and snakeskin and take to the floor. I felt like Elizabeth Taylor in *Giant* when they serve her the barbecued brains: a little overwhelmed by the ritual.

Then there was the benefit at Liberace's old house, a gilt-edged manse with flocked wallpaper and a fine view of other people's backyards. In every room was a piano, and at every piano was an artiste recruited from the cocktail bars, rehearsal halls, and orchestra pits of the city. A few hours into the event, at precisely the same moment—whether by design or chance, we will never know—every single one of them was somewhere in the middle of "Send in the Clowns." Fellini would have been elbowed out of the way by Busby Berkeley.

I did a benefit on ice last year. It was for Sheila Kuehl, the former star of *The Many Loves of Dobie Gillis* who is now doing battle as an openly gay California legislator. Everyone sat shivering in their parkas in full view of the 80-degree weather outside and watched former Ice Capettes do their time-honored routines (will the girl at the end be able to catch up with the ever-spinning line of other girls?).

Sheila and I did another benefit, this one for Outfest, the Los Angeles gay and lesbian film festival, and we did it with Margarethe Cammermeyer, Armistead Maupin, and Julie Newmar. We were each asked to choose one lousy movie we saw early in life that helped make us the people we are today. The series was called "Guilty Pleasures." Armistead and I evidently were the only ones who read the manual. I chose *There's No Business Like Show Business,* a great big cow chip of a musical that I adored as a kid, and he went for *Bell, Book, and Candle,* with Kim Novak chanting to her Siamese cat. Sheila chose *A Star Is Born* (the great Judy version), Greta chose *Yentl* (from the executive producer who brought her story to television), and Julie dragged in *Some Like It Hot.* How could they have gotten this so wrong? But, hey, it's a benefit.

In the last month I've also been to two pool benefits, one of them actually in a pool and the other where you shoot pool. Shooting *in* a pool has not yet been proposed as a fund-raiser, although I have presided over a gay-porno awards banquet, which is probably the closest thing. I worked as closely as possible with a lot of people named Chad, Ty, Zack, and Kevin, and it's been just about my favorite benefit so far. The beneficiary was a very small AIDS charity, so lean that ninety-three cents on every dollar actually goes to people with AIDS. This had a fitting irony, as ninety-three cents of every dollar I make goes to people named Chad, Ty, Zack, and Kevin. You can't even commit sins in charity's name anymore.

# Trailer Trash

Ellen is staring at me from the cover of *Time*, dressed just a little bit like a Heaven's Gate cult member, declaring, "Yep, I'm gay." And up in the corner the magazine is plugging another story:"The Backlash Against HOMOS." Jesus . . . *already?* I look again. I've misread. It's "The Backlash Against HMOs." Whew. That was a close one.

Well, you can't blame me. These are exciting times for homosexuals as well as for insurance agents. Homosexual insurance agents must be dancing in place. Everywhere you turn you can hear the sounds of barriers crashing down as we flood our way into the mainstream. Classic foes like Jerry Falwell pipe up with the tired old "promoting the gay lifestyle" line, and nouveau pains in the ass like Camille Paglia even offer him some support. But the mass of straight Americans who have been exposed to us know we're more than a style—we're a life, albeit, a life filled with extreme style.

Of course, it's easier to be gay in San Francisco than in Topeka, Kan., but with twenty-four gay characters on prime-time television and with as familiar and unthreatening a presence as Ellen DeGeneres gracing the cover of *Time*—shucks, it's got to be getting easier.

In such heady times—with everyone marching around holding his or her feathers up proudly—it's always a blow to find that dragons are lurking in waters we used to think safe. Just the other day in user-friendly West Hollywood, Calif., I ducked into the octoplex to play hooky at the movies. I settled into my seat, burrowed into my popcorn, and began to watch the endless series of previews without which no octoplex is complete. You probably haven't noticed, but the previews, known as "trailers" in the trade, are rated just like movies.

I'd never noticed this either because most trailers get G ratings, which means they can be shown with any movie you can throw at them. However, every now and again a trailer gets an R rating, which means it can be shown only with an R-rated movie. You'll notice these trailers because the rating is splashed across a screen that has been colored blood-red for the occasion. Such a warning flashed across the screen before a trailer for the film *Chasing Amy*.

This is a sweet little romantic comedy about a guy who falls for a girl and discovers that she's interested only in other girls. The trailer shows, for an instant, two girls kissing. There is no violence, no sex, no guns, no blood, no drug use, no torture, and no bad language in the trailer.

Other trailers shown before and after the *Chasing Amy* preview featured such clean family values as small children being threatened by dinosaurs, men being eaten by insect aliens, men with big guns blowing away other men with big guns, and lots of people screaming as the cars they are riding in head for cliffs. These trailers were all rated G. Other than the lesbian kiss, there was nothing anyone could possibly object to in the trailer for *Chasing Amy*. Yet it—and only it—got the warning label.

I called a friend at the Motion Picture Association of America, which administers movie ratings; my friend said the organization never comments on the way it assigns ratings. Then I called a friend in the trailer business. She listened patiently and told me the material in the *Chasing Amy* trailer sounded MPAA-objectionable on "thematic" grounds. "This is an outfit that takes what it considers a 'parent's-eye view,'" she said. "In the eyes of most parents, a lesbian kiss is something they don't want their kids to see when the kids have been parked at the matinee of *One Hundred and One Dalmatians*. Giving the trailer an R rating ensures that it will not be shown with a G-rated picture. It's the only guarantee they have."

OK. I can understand the rating part, to keep objectionable things away from kids. What I can't understand is what they consider objectionable, especially in light of what they consider acceptable. Which parents are the MPAA representing? The ones on their way to the NRA picnic? Surely not the millions who watched *20/20*'s unbelievably positive coverage of Melissa Etheridge and Julie Cypher's new baby. Surely not the ones who are young enough to be giving birth. No one born in the '70s can be that square and unaware. Or can they? You mean we still have work to do? Ellen isn't enough? Help! Mommy!

**Look Who's Talking**

What happened at the Hotel Honolulu will not go down in the history books. It won't have to, because the guests have already written the books. And what they've written is a diary of gay life over the past fifteen years. If you cruise the back pages of this publication, you've probably seen the ads for the hotel—the only open, avowed, self-confessed, acknowledged homo hostelry on Oahu (or Oa'hu, as it is now known; the Hawaiians are trying to revive their language by bringing back all the slashes, dashes, and umlauts they gave up to the white devil).

*Oa'hu* means "gathering place," and *Honolulu* means "fair harbor," and for some time now the hotel has functioned as the former for the latter, especially if you add a *y* to *fair*. Coupled with the legendary Hula's Bar and Lei Stand, whose double entendre never fails to pulverize malihinis (that's "newcomers"), this square block in the middle of Waikiki has served as a mid-Pacific mecca for years. This may all change soon, as the Asian tourist boom that has turned nearby Kalakaua Avenue into a glass canyon of high-rises and shopping malls threatens to engulf and devour everything in its path. Already the faux-deco Polynesian movie palace, the Kuhio (where Bette Midler worked as an usherette) is gone, to be replaced by Nike Town. The hotel can't be far behind.

But if the place does go, its secrets will not die with it. Management has seen to that. When you check into the Hotel Honolulu, in addition to the rattan furniture and ceiling fans you get a strange, shaded lanai-balcony-patio arrangement outside your front door. There's a chair out there and a writing table. And on the writing table is one of those black-and-white-patterned composition books they used to have in grade schools (by now they must have composition computers). *Hmm,* you think, *the last guest must have left this.* Indeed he did. He left it for you. And so did the guest before him, and the guest before him, all the way back to guest zero.

Since 1983, guests have been jotting down their impressions, their adventures, their complaints, their worldviews, and, occasionally, their phone numbers on the mainland. The entries are astonishingly dense, written in longhand, often above, below, and around dark stains of unknown origin.

Protected by their anonymity, the ghosts of guests past unburden themselves of their memories. Forget the latest Kitty Kelley; this is the real stuff. If the walls could talk . . . well, hey, they're talking. Some of the entries in my room's diary made me want to call down to housekeeping and make sure the mattress had been turned. People had apparently had sex on the dresser, in the sink, in the shower, in the closet, on the north-facing wall, and in bed (oh, that old thing), sometimes without stopping for commercials. My room seemed to be the favorite of a lot of military types. Why, I don't know. Don't ask, don't tell. But someone was always leaving his hat or his crop or his wings and had to come back the next day.

I put the book down and gingerly felt my way to the bathroom. My psychic friend who exercises his powers by touching things would have been in the ER by now, hyperventilating into a paper bag. I barely made it to the john before I remembered one especially choice thing that'd happened there. Of course, that was back in 1986, but still . . . I flipped around some more. Not all the reminiscences were sexual. Some were actual prose poems about the beauty of the islands. Some talked about how the town was being ruined by developers. One talked poignantly about going to Pearl Harbor to visit the resting place of a grandfather.

The temperature of our outlaw society went up and down with each passing era. The wildest entries were the earliest; then there was a period when a lot of twelve-steppers seemed to be checking in, and still later the references moved from sex to drugs. Many a K-hole was created in my room. There was a period during which people who were about to die came to Hawaii to have one last stab at life. And more recently people who thought they were going to die but now find they're not are coming to Hawaii to figure out what to do with their lives.

The next wave of visitors, of course, will be the most interesting and least expected of all. The honeymooners. They'll have a hard time topping some of the antics that went before. But at least some of what they're doing will be legal.

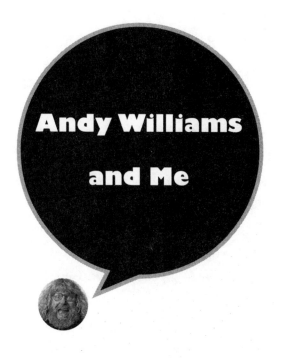

# Andy Williams and Me

The last closet in show business is in Branson, MO. "I can't wait for them to get a load of you here," Andy Williams told me on the phone. We were chatting as I steered my rented full-size toward Branson, a strip of highway in the middle of the Ozarks where thirty-seven—count 'em, thirty-seven—Vegas-style showroom theaters light up every morning, noon, and night to entertain tourists who come from, literally, God only knows where.

I was going to check out Andy's show, for which I had actually written some material. Here was a chance to see how I played in Peoria, or worse. Andy does his two-hour Broadway-Hollywood extravaganza twice a day from April through October in his own Moon River Theater. "Are there any gay bars?" I asked the straight but always-hip Andy.

"God, no. I don't think there are even any gay chorus boys here." Think again, Andy. "Well, there was one," he added. "He was in my show. But he quit. He got tired of driving to Springfield every time he wanted to go dancing."

For a town with no gay chorus boys, Branson does have its share of *Advocate* readers. I was greeted—quietly—by several of them at virtually every place I stopped: at the Roy Rogers restaurant, which is the best in town; at the spectacular Lake of the Ozarks; and at the Holiday Inn, which, at four stories, is Branson's tallest structure. The second tallest structure is Erma Grundfest, a waitress at Roy Rogers, who is a local landmark on par with the HOLLYWOOD sign.

Branson is a show business burial ground that rivals Forest Lawn, but as Andy likes to point out, the cemetery plots are lined with gold. His theater, which is only slightly less elaborate than the Metropolitan Opera House, is a smash hit of nearly a decade. Tony Orlando is a big name in Branson. Other variety show vets like Wayne Newton and Mel Tillis have anchored there with varying degrees of success.

The crowd tends to spill off buses, and there are, no doubt, a lot of fundamentalists milling about, but being a good Christian evidently doesn't guarantee big box office. Anita Bryant—anybody old enough to remember her?—was reduced to playing 11 A.M. shows, when nothing else is happening. Even with that, she was forced to pack up her snake oil and slither out of town.

The biggest attraction, bigger even than Andy, is a Japanese fiddle player–entertainer named Shoji Tobuchi, who is married to a spectacular blonde who sings and dances and shows off their children. A bigger attraction than Shoji is the men's room at his theater, which has been decorated to closely resemble some of the larger sets from *The King and I*. Tour buses stop just to check out the decor.

The town is a great American paradox, splashily celebrating God and country but fueled by the savvy, campy energy that drives Broadway, Hollywood, and Vegas. Even Andy's most recent show featured the star all fruited up as Carmen Miranda for the venerable Manilow number "Copacabana." The bus riders shrieked with delight, and only a tragic lack of forethought prevented staff from selling Andy/Carmen action figures at the souvenir shop. Those responsible have been sent back to the Castro.

You'd think any show business mecca the size of Branson—thirty-seven theaters, nudging London!—would be rife with chapters of all your favorite organizations, from Avatar (for the leather lover) to the Xenaphiles. But Andy is right. The phrase *low profile* takes on a bizarre, Herve Villechaize dimension in Branson. Nervous giggles and furtive glances are still in style.

A gay sensibility informs all the entertainment and at least a third of the employment opportunities, but there is no gay life to speak of. It's like Disneyland, where you know all those fresh-faced kids pretending to be fairy-tale characters are dancing around in Madonna cone bras the moment they shut their lockers. Except even Disneyland has its Gay Nights.

I don't think the city fathers of Branson are cooking up one of those, much less a pride parade. There are all the usual reasons for this. Branson is not a theme park, after all, but a town in the middle notch in the Bible Belt. Gay people have traditionally not had a presence in the area. But then, neither has Big Time Show Biz, until now. It will be interesting to see what develops over in the Ozarks. Who knows? A couple of years from now, you may be able to marry your gay cousin.

# Partying
# for Pride

Gay pride's bustin' out all over. By the time you read this, there will have been lavish parades replete with drag queens, porn stars, local politicians, Motown has-beens, hordes of lesbian gynecologists marching in lockstep, buffed numbers snaking out of their Speedos as they dance with abandon high atop papier-mâché representations of the Emerald City. If this sounds like the ringmaster's spiel at Ringling Bros., that's because a circus is a circus, no matter how you dress it up. No minority as theatrical as ours could be expected to celebrate itself with anything less than a show business extravaganza.

Could it? Sure, we show up for serious-minded marches on Washington. But it's the parades and the weekends where we really pat ourselves on the ass . . . I mean, back. It's all dutifully covered by the media. To their credit, where they used to show only the bechained and beplumed, they've now gotten around to focusing on PFLAG contingents and beaming politicos in our midst. The TV audience gets some sense of balance, I suppose. Except we all know that TV is about images, and we remember the wild ones.

I used to have a big thing about gay pride parades. They struck me as tacky pseudoevents—Mardi Gras for people who couldn't get to New Orleans. They were a terrific excuse for people to get drunk and throw up in the middle of the afternoon. They were a great place to show off newly acquired abs, cutoffs, and boyfriends. Performers whose big talent was that they were openly gay got to strut their stuff for probably the biggest crowds they would ever encounter. Purveyors of crappy jewelry and incense burners could take a day off from the swap meets, raise their prices, and appeal to lesbians and gay men as if they were doing us a favor by selling us remainders that had fallen off a truck in Taiwan.

Couples who otherwise maintained a discreet distance in public could go topless and deep-tongue each other. People who were so thoroughly into their alternative lifestyle that they couldn't appear anywhere ordinary without being harassed would come out of their warrens to display all their piercings, tattoos, and torture devices turned into necklaces and bracelets.

"It wasn't like this in the old days," I would murmur as I skulked around, sidestepping the rivers of God-knows-what oozing down the street. Why, when I was an itty-bitty queen, back before Stonewall, there wasn't any pride, but by whillikers, there was dignity. We hid in dark bars listening to Judy Garland records, wondering if anybody was safe to come on to or if every other person in the room was a vice cop. We spoke in code. You weren't out, you weren't even gay—you were a friend of Dorothy. You wore a red kerchief in your back left pocket or a blue kerchief in your right: I couldn't remember which, which explains some early bruises.

We all had short hair and wore ties, the concept being not to call attention to yourself. "Sissy" was what you didn't want to be. Yet bodybuilders were the only ones who had bodies. There were no periodontists with pecs. If there were lipstick lesbians, they pretty much stuck to the cosmetics counters at the smaller drugstores. "Mannish" was a polite way of casting doubt on a woman's sexuality. So there was no pride, but there was the glamour of a shared secret, and that kept many a miserable invert going. The self-hatred that came with the burden of maintaining the secret also did more than a few of them in.

The world began changing after Stonewall, of course, and later it changed again when we galvanized around the issue of AIDS. A group that has suffered so much loss needs to remind itself it still exists. So we celebrate survival, which we translate into pride.

Every Jewish holiday (and I celebrate them all) can be described thusly: They persecuted us. We beat them. Let's eat. Gay pride is the same thing, except instead of eating, we substitute . . . oh, what the hell. Show the world where you've pierced yourself. You've earned it. Just save me a bottle of whatever beer we're not boycotting.

# Breaking the Code

This will come as a shock to some of you, but many years ago there was another Donny and Marie show, nothing like the one that's on now. I was one of the writers. We had ice-skaters and confetti and movie parodies in which Marie was Dorothy, Donny was the Scarecrow, and Paul Lynde was the Wicked Witch of the West. He spent all week tormenting the Munchkins by putting their lunch trays on a high shelf. Emmys?

Never. But we had a few good years, and then *The Incredible Hulk* wiped us off the map.

One of the favorite games the writers used to play was getting a suggestive lyric past the ABC censors or, even tougher, the Mormon elders who used to scrutinize every script. (The Osmonds, in case you missed the memo, are devout Mormons who, at least in those days, built their shows around strict church guidelines; to this day, every time I see Orrin Hatch on TV, I think he's waiting for me to hand him script pages.)

I considered it a great personal victory when I got Marie to sing "Don't Let the Sun Go Down on Me" and nobody objected. But that was topped mere months later when, in an effort to declare herself a solo artist not always linked to her brother, she opened the show with the Diana Ross hit "I'm Coming Out."

"Oh, doesn't that make ya wanna weep? Marie is coming out," Lynde remarked dryly from the wings. "I knew it was just a matter of time." We shared a laugh, that secret laugh that gay people don't share much anymore.

Coming out is not only a national pastime, but now it's also a national holiday. Back then, of course, people didn't publicly admit they were gay unless they were being led away in handcuffs and couldn't deny it. Even a decade after Stonewall, the phrase *coming out* didn't have a lot of mainstream circulation. Could you imagine Diana Ross singing a song about it if it did?

We had more secret phrases in our closet than we had gaily colored kerchiefs, but they all worked the same way. The phrases told you the lay of the land about a person's sexuality. The kerchief, worn in the right place, told you how to lay him. We were a secret society, damn it, and we had a secret code.

Ground zero was always *The Wizard of Oz*. Somebody wasn't gay, he was "a friend of Dorothy." Happy souls would tell you he was "festive." Gloomier friends would describe him as being "in the life." Perhaps he "liked show tunes." Queenier types were solemnly described as "a member of the royal order of the lavender."

Whole conversations could be built in code. "Does he play in our band?" "Oh, yes. And, you know, he's in real estate. He's got a big piece of property in the valley." "No kidding. Just looking at him, I knew he was musical. Maybe he'll do that flute solo." And no one else in the elevator knew what you were talking about.

Lesbians had codes of their own, of course. I was doing a benefit at the Metropolitan Opera once, and a noted diva took the stage. One of the sound engineers turned to me and winked. "Break out your scuba gear. It's time to dive."

In the pre-Stonewall days, *gay* could still mean lighthearted and carefree, so if you saw somebody you thought might be, you could always ask something quasi-innocent like "I'm going to Columbus, Ohio. Are there any gay places there?" The answer got you your answer. Once we co-opted the word and used it to label our entire culture, that little conversational ploy fell w-a-a-ay out of fashion.

Amazingly, a whole raft of coded words has found its way into the mainstream. Does anyone ever say something is "in the closet" without smiling? Farmers in Iowa know that "drag" is more than what the tractor does. I've heard straight suburban types refer to other straight suburban types as "drama queens." Modern moms chuckle when their little girls dress as fairies (less so when their little boys do; some habits die hard).

And probably nothing will ever top the legend that is carved across the proscenium of the Goodman Theatre of Chicago; YOU YOURSELF, it tells the audience, MUST SET FIRE TO THE FAGOTS YOU HAVE BROUGHT. Wait a minute, that's not code. That's just English. Wow, a whole other language to explore.

# The Absolutely Fabulous British

I have just joined the ranks of Quentin Crisp, Noël Coward, the queen mother, and other notable queens and mothers. I was interviewed this week by the BBC. It was for a series its creators are calling *Men in Hollywood*. The British are fond of Hollywood (and notoriously fond of men). The British tend to revere lots of things Americans dismiss. Hollywood is, natch, at the top of that list.

The other night I saw the controversial new movie *Priest,* the most interesting aspect of which by far was the fact that this young Liverpool cleric could quote Tammy Wynette lyrics by heart. How many American priests could do that? Anyway, the Brits have invaded lotusland with a full camera crew, and they are barreling o'er hill and beach, piecing together one of those four-part docus that will no doubt wind up on public broadcasting stations (if Newt lets them live) during pledge week.

The thrust of the show seems to be that while the plight of women in Hollywood has been painstakingly examined, no one has addressed the state of men as, I don't know, a voting bloc? A workforce? A demographic? Don't men, even though we all know they're the group in power, have internecine struggles, peer pressure, performance anxiety, manly concerns?

Leave it to British TV to grapple with these issues while *Vanity Fair* is busy putting every actress in Hollywood on its cover in some form of underwear or other. Just in case I thought they were going to break new ground, however, our cousins from across the Big Pond asked the first question everybody asks: Is there a casting couch for men? Baby, give me the address! If there is such a thing in Hollywood, it's probably just a love seat. And it's tucked away in the corner of some sad little office in a strip mall in the San Fernando Valley and belongs to a guy who doesn't have enough guts to get into porn but lures lads who've just fallen off the turnip truck.

And what about women in power? Any woman with enough clout to use her job for sex would find her enemies—and they are circling her constantly with the grim patience of hammerheads—all too eager to use this ammunition against her. It would be stupid, Eve, easy to expose, not worthy of you.

Gay men with enough power to use sex as a bargaining chip find they really can't. Any handsome young man they put forth as a "discovery" immediately falls under this veil of suspicion. Actors don't want to be put under this veil, so the serious, talented ones don't mess around. They don't have to. The marginal ones might, but it doesn't get them anywhere. They remain marginal. As largely do the men they mess around with.

There are exceptions to this rule, of course. Everybody has an example of a major star who has gone this route. Now that we are deep into the activist '90s, it would seem that the veil of suspicion would be about ready to blow away. And it's true that if enough romantic leading men—the kind who are so frequently expected to get the girl—came out, the perceived media poison of being gay and romantic might just evaporate.

I've always maintained that we are in the illusion business out here, and the audience needs to feel that it's plausible for the romantic leads to wind up together. Too much information about either of them, and the illusion is shattered. Maybe. I'd love for someone to test that theory. But the kind of bravery I am asking of an actor may be beyond an actor's scope. Actors are, after all, people who make a living trying to disappear into someone else's skin. If they were totally comfortable in their own, they probably wouldn't be doing this.

On I go in this vein, and I notice the British crew making little mime gestures about how it's almost time for tea and is this rump-sprung Muppet ever going to shut up? So I let them ask the next question. Is there a gay mafia? I assume they mean in Hollywood, because if there were one hanging around the Corleone compound, jeez, would they have some stories to tell. What they mean by this, of course, is, Aren't there a bunch of powerful gay men at the top of the Hollywood pyramid; and aren't they making decisions affecting art, life, and culture; and aren't they in some sort of collusion when they make these decisions? This amuses me, especially coming from the Brits, because they usually ask this same question about Jews; so it was interesting to see how the same old suede pump was being slid over a brand-new foot.

The truth is, there's a handful of meaningfully powerful gay men in Hollywood, and only a couple of them are even out. They may hang around one another's pools, they may have swapped a phone number or two, and they may have even have sought one another's counsel now and again. But they do very little as a group that affects what all of us see on the screen.

And here is where the interviewer won me back. Wouldn't it be nice, she said, if they did? If they all got together and used their collective power to promote one gay action hero or one lesbian sex symbol? If they offered enough cushion and support to allow one leading actor to be as brave as his heart tells him to be? In the face of such a brilliant, modest proposal, what could I say? Rule, Britannia! And does anyone have Prince Edward's private line?

# Waiting to Expire

I went to see *Waiting to Exhale* in Miami Beach, where about two-thirds of the audience were waiting to expire. Long known as God's Waiting Room, the little sandspit across the bay is experiencing the kind of renaissance the Medicis would have enjoyed, and they would really have liked to get their hands on some of the drugs. In the lower half of town, South Beach, everybody who isn't gay is Eurotrash, and everybody who isn't

Eurotrash is Latin and a print model, and everybody who isn't Latin and a print model is an old Jew wandering around wondering why all these people are making all this noise all of a sudden. Oy.

Just to liven things up, every now and again one of those sexual Ringling Brothers shows called a circuit party arrives in town, and thousands of boys from all walks of life descend for a weekend bacchanal, the theme of which is something really profound, like "White."

People stay up all night and crowd the movie houses by day, which is wise ever since we found out that melanoma is not our friend. So it was that several hundred of them got to experience *Waiting to Exhale* with several hundred Miami Beach old-timers, and when we talk old-timer in Miami Beach, we're talking *old*. There were so many people with walkers that, for the moment before they opened the doors, a casual passerby might actually have thought that somebody was staging a race. Popcorn sales were light because not many in the crowd could still chew. The gay boys had bought every item containing sugar, so pickings at the concession stand were slim.

The picture was delayed while everyone got seated and reseated and rereseated. The trailer for *Nixon* drew shrieks of laughter from the gay crowd (for camp intensity it rivals *Mommie Dearest*) but—get this—there were loud, hacking, vociferous boos from the old-timers. They always hated Nixon, these retired northern liberal Democrats. And they may have forgotten their phone numbers, but they remember how much they hated him.

Then *Waiting to Exhale* came on—a picture in which the entire cast is black and middle- to upper-middle-class and no one ever says "nigger." But they do say "faggot" four times. We shall overcome, indeed. To be fair, it's a teenager who says it, and his mother tells him to watch his language. She could have told him more, but she doesn't. There were no boos from our crowd or any other crowd, but by then I suspect they'd been narcotized by the beautiful sunsets and the beautiful music and the beautiful women.

The men aren't bad either; but, of course, this is a picture about four women, so the men have to embody everything that's wrong with their lives. There isn't much else wrong. These gals greet every day with a full face of makeup and the sort of drag Ross Hunter would have green-lighted with enthusiasm for any Doris Day picture. It would have spiced things up if one of them had been a lesbian, but that kind of bonding is outside the scope of this film.

Instead, bisexuality is introduced via an ex-husband who returns to confess all to the mother of his child, then leaves again. While the ex-wife, played charmingly by Loretta Devine, never holds it against him, it plays disappointingly into the tenor of male-bashing that defines the movie. Bisexuality is something else that's wrong with men. Although to a straight woman, I suppose, it legitimately *is*. Duh.

The bonding goes on and on in *Waiting to Exhale*. It's a sort of *Fried Chocolate Tomatoes*. There has been a spate of gay plays and films lately that touch on bonding, but the bonding doesn't seem to be about being gay. It's generally about experiencing loss. For pure gay bonding all we have is Gay Pride Month. And we're not terribly kind to one another after that.

When the last Whitney-Aretha-Chaka shriek had been shruk and the movie was ending, the crowd made its creaky, lumbering way into hot, humid daylight. The smokers, who had spent two hours waiting to inhale, elbowed their way to the sidewalk. And then I noticed something: Some of the people with walkers—in fact, quite a few of the people with walkers—were not old-timers at all. They were new-timers. They were gay men in various stages of AIDS-related illnesses. You don't see them much at night in Miami Beach, which is when the whirl of trend is at its windiest. At night everybody on South Beach is twenty-two and just got here six months ago from Des Moines or Minneapolis or Kansas City. It's what San Francisco was like in the '70s, the period chronicled so brilliantly by Armistead Maupin in *Tales of the City*.

By day you notice that not everybody on South Beach is twenty-two. They may have just gotten here, but many of them have come because it is the home of the last party, and they want to party because otherwise they will spend the rest of their time on earth just waiting to exhale.

In this regard they are like the retirees who came before

them. And the retirees know this. They live in the same build-ings, shop in the same markets, and, on this bright afternoon, go to the same movies and help one another out the door. It's bonding, and it's worth noting, because it will probably never make it into the big-time movie.

Lana Turner died the same day Hugh Grant was arrested. The way I figure it, Lana spent the whole day watching the coverage. It wasn't much, but it beat that day's O.J. session, which was right up there with Margaret Thatcher interviews for tempo and excitement. Every time one of the stations went "in-depth" with Hugh, they discovered there was about as much depth to the case as one of the slimmer Sidney Sheldon novels. So they began dredging up famous Hollywood superstar scandals of the past, and of course, it didn't take them long to land on Lana.

You will remember—OK, some of you will remember—that on Easter weekend of 1958, Lana's teenage daughter came home and found her mother engaged in another slugfest with her gangster boyfriend, Johnny Stompanato, whose name simultaneously described his personal style and his career choice. Blinded by passion and rage, the girl stabbed Stompanato, and he died on the floor of the Beverly Hills home he had terrorized for some years. The trial was the kind of sensation we used to produce in this country only every once in a while, not every day the way we do now. Lana on the witness stand—we had to go to the movies and see it in newsreels for the full effect—was something to behold, especially for those of us for whom the line between a larger-than-life image and a larger-than-life reality was being crossed for the very first time.

What a figure Lana cut, her movie-star sunglasses, her mussed hairdo, her ruined makeup. She was that girl she played in *The Bad and the Beautiful,* plus a bit of Mrs. Norman Maine, a touch of Mildred Pierce, an echo of Julie Jordan in *Carousel.* But she was also a real mother, a real battered woman, a real victim. As I said, the line had been crossed.

Lana's tragedy became popular fiction, inspiring Harold Robbins's novel *Where Love Has Gone,* which was turned into a true trash classic starring—brace yourself—Susan Hayward and Joey Heatherton in the mother-daughter roles. A short while back Woody Allen even explored the case thirty years down the road in *September,* in which he had the thirty-years-older pair played by—now really brace yourself—Elaine Stritch and Mia Farrow. But that one bombed, and even though everyone involved in the case, including both Lana and her daughter, wrote memoirs, the whole thing had more or less faded into the yellow-edged oblivion of a once-juicy story.

That is, until Hugh Grant. All day the reporters cranked out the story, and all day they compared it with Lana. My theory is that Lana decided to be rid of all of us. If, after all this time, they were going to take her very real tragedy and stack it up against Hugh's dreary little escapade, there really wasn't much reason to go on. When her daughter says, "She just took a breath and was gone," I think it was Lana's way of saying "Enough!"

Who can blame her? Lana's scandal seems to be outliving her work, not because of the quality of the work but because basically we're more interested in scandal. Enough has not been enough for quite a while now. Hugh Grant will have to make some pretty big pictures if he doesn't wish to be forever remembered as the john of the '90s (though he would have to spend another $53,440 to match Charlie Sheen's record).

Of course, as the pundits pund, it could have been worse. For a while, it was. First reports had it that Ms. Divine Brown was a preop. You can see the *Current Affair* coverage now—THE HOOKER HAD A HARD-ON! Phones were ringing off the wall (or wherever people keep phones now), and the implications were staggering. Had Hugh intentionally sought out a boy? Or had he been fooled like so many before him by those cagey Sunset Boulevard cross-dressers? How could we be sure? The police released a photo of Divine, but the hard core were still unconvinced. For a few frenzied hours, every Hollywood newshound and bitch I know was calling me—*moi!*—to "find out what you know about this guy's history." Suddenly I'm the resident don at Hugh U.

Finally, people who knew Divine came forward and put out the fire, and a certain segment of the Hollywood publicity machine breathed a very silent sigh of relief. Because a faithless Hugh Grant was easier to spin than a gay Hugh Grant. The image of Britain's toothiest light comedian forgetting about his glamorous girlfriend for a momentary fling with Cleopatra Jones was infinitely more palatable than the prospect of his leaving Elizabeth Hurley for twenty minutes with RuPaul.

Still, a faction of the press corps wasn't satisfied with Hugh's heterosexuality. There had to be something more to all this, more than just Little Hugh telling Big Hugh to pull over at the next stoplight. He had to have a darker purpose, a deeper secret, something more to hide. He couldn't throw his life away for *this*. It began sounding like the plot of an old Gordon Merrick novel or Dirk Bogarde in *Victim*.

In the interim Lana Turner died, and absolutely no one

mentioned that her daughter, Cheryl Crane, is an out lesbian activist. At one time this would have been big news. It has evidently worn out its sensationalist appeal. In the depths of the sewer, a tiny beam of sunshine does now and again break through.

It's Our

Party

Greetings from planet party. That's what it's like this time of the year. Nobody seems to be on duty anywhere. The Republicans and the Democrats are both busy having bashes. The Atlanta Olympics were a huge bacchanal. Provincetown, Rehoboth Beach, Laguna Beach—the season's preeminent dick docks— are bursting with revelers. The bushes of Fire Island are busier than the Bushes of the GOP. According to a puzzling mailer from Air France, most of which had to do with the exciting new angle of sleeper seats in *classe d'affaires,* 75 percent of all Parisians will leave Paris in August. (Their places will promptly be filled by Americans.)

Everybody's uncorking the deep-frying and watching aliens get whupped at the movies. (Would it have killed them to have made Harvey Fierstein a fighter pilot? Every other minority got its shot.) Even Disney, in marketing its animated Broadway musical version of *The Hunchback of Notre Dame,* used the slogan "Join the party!" Would that be the garroting party or the flogging party? By the time you have finished reading this, there will have been a White Party, a Black Party, a Mauve-and-Magenta Party, a Morning Party, an AIDS benefit where you jump in a pool, and a vegetarian barbecue where some enterprising caterer tries to pass off tofu sausages as the real thing (from the folks who brought you dildos).

It was during such a hot, mindless summer twenty-seven years ago that the nightly party at the Stonewall bar turned into the small riot that changed the gay world forever. Of course, the parties weren't organized then in any but a symbolic sense. The bar, park, or tearoom you went to; the color handkerchief you wore; the precise pocket you wore it in—these were the symbols, and this was a lot of the gay world.

For variety there was the Mattachine Society, which some recognized as the first stirrings of a gay political movement but which many of us regarded as an innovative way to meet intellectual-type guys. Guilty as charged. Mattachine comes in for some pretty amusing characterization in *Stonewall,* the current movie whose skirts are loosely gathered around Martin Duberman's memoir of the riot and its period. The early members are depicted as uptight, hairless, bespectacled, and yet possessed of an almost unearthly courage and determination. Marching around as if they were hippies or blacks or both, they demanded equal rights for homosexuals, not gays or queers— we hadn't come up with those angles yet. No one much noticed them, and even the movie seems ambivalent about them, bestowing its lavender seal of approval on the riotous drag queens who, after all, did make the first tiny squeak on the wheel that became the liberation movement.

*Stonewall,* even with its weird sidetracks into personal stories that seem as if they came out of another movie, is a fascinating picture with some wonderfully compelling actors in its leads. Watching it, you're led to believe that what went on in the tortured social lives of these drag queens was basically what was going on in all of gay life. This is not exactly the case. At the exact same time that Stonewall was happening, Mart Crowley's landmark play *The Boys in the Band* was enjoying a smash success off-Broadway. It was also about a party, the kind of Night of the Long Knives that Edward Albee had made so popular in *Who's Afraid of Virginia Woolf?* The guests at Crowley's do were all very Upper East Side. Even the black guy had been raised in the great house where his mother worked as a servant. Everybody seemed to be well educated and making a fine living, and, well, that was the point of it. On the surface, the boys in the band—those faceless fellows who were always supporting the star—were just like everyone else. You couldn't tell them apart. But just underneath, the differences were palpable. The levels of trauma and self-hatred and so forth that mark the characters are a source of debate that comes up every time the play is revived, as it has been this year in New York.

But the world depicted in it did exist, and it was a world apart from Stonewall. Occasionally the two spheres collided, usually at the end of a very druggy evening. And then the real party would begin. However, in the category of Gay Parties for a Hundred, Alex, undoubtedly the most unexpected entry ever is *It's My Party,* which is just emerging on videocassette. More than loosely based on director Randal Kleiser's own experiences when his ex-lover died, it's about a man facing imminent AIDS vegetation who decides to throw his own farewell fete, at the end of which he will descend into a very personal production of *The Big Sleep.*

Now we're talking *party.* Many people have criticized the movie because it's about Hollywood types who live well, as if that somehow makes their AIDS suffering less emotionally wrenching. That's like saying Pharaoh's anguish over the death of his firstborn couldn't compare with the anguish of the assistant hieroglyph chipper over the death of his firstborn. Grow up. *It's My Party* and *Stonewall* and *The Boys in the Band* are all about gay men at the end of their rope. They don't all survive, but they all leave survivors who move forward armed with some new, vital knowledge. I wish more parties wound up like that.

**Public Access to Gays**

It's a really big night on TV. David Duchovny, the *X-Files* hunk-ette who made a lot of noise by wearing a red Speedo in the pilot, is pretending to maybe (maybe not) be gay on the season premiere of *The Larry Sanders Show*. Ellen DeGeneres is announcing on promos that her character is coming out, but what she means is that her boobs are coming out of her dress. Ellen DeGeneres showing boobs and wearing a dress is probably bigger news than character Ellen Morgan coming out. The gay cop who left *NYPD Blue* to be a gay cop on *Public Morals* is now a gay cop without a beat because the network removed life-support systems from the struggling new show after a record-shattering single episode.

Over on the Learning Channel, a series called *Great Country Inns* is doing half an hour on another in what appears to be an inexhaustible supply of Russian River bed-and-breakfasts run by earnest lesbian couples. The girls rise at dawn, churn their own butter, bake their own scones, and set a lovely table for the honeymooning straight guests who have spent a long night kicking holes in the walls and breaking three of the four posts on every quaint feather bed in the joint. While Sandy does the repair work, Kelly throws together a picnic-basket lunch and spends several hours defoliating the riverbank to create a centerpiece the size of Mount Tamalpais. Soon it's time for the ol' pasta machine to get cranking, and before long Sandy and Kelly are winking and nudging as the honeymoon couples polish off a bottle of wine and stagger back upstairs for another round. No intimation of where the girls will spend the night.

On *Saturday Night Live* the latest cartoon caper is "The Ambiguously Gay Duo," about two superhero crime fighters with pouches big enough to house medium-size kangaroos. They drive a hugely phallic car to the scene of every crime and invariably wind up in each other's arms, usually to save each other from a flaming pit or some such. It's at this point that they notice that the supervillains are studying them intently for signs of gayness. "What are you looking at?" they demand.

"Nothing!" the supervillains hastily reply.

A polite middle-class gay couple got married last season on *Roseanne,* and a polite middle-class lesbian couple did ditto on *Friends.* This is what is happening on network TV. The much-dreaded mainstreaming of gay America is quietly taking place. The worst fears of lesbians and gay men—that we will be outcast because we have been demonized—are slowly subsiding. The worst fears of the homophobic right—that we will be accepted because we have not been demonized enough—are slowly becoming real. The television establishment, faced with the inevitability of gay people declaring themselves, has taken great steps to assimilate us into the consumerist middle class, just as they have every other ethnic group. We are now routinely depicted as slightly exotic variations of the folks next door.

You want to see kinky sex, alternative lifestyles, fringe political groups, airheads who claim they have found the cure for AIDS—in other words, much of the stuff the reactionary right claims to be frightened of? Get your trench coat and your hat and channel-surf your way over to public access. After years of coaxing even local news organizations into highlighting more than just bikers and drag queens in their coverage of our community, we may have thought the screen had been blanched of our more flamboyant components. But, as the chaos theorist in *Jurassic Park* is fond of observing, life will find a way.

When cable TV arrived, Congress—or someone—thoughtfully decided that a nice trade-off for suddenly making us pay for TV would be to give us, the public, our own channel. So for like twenty-five bucks, any one of us can rent half an hour of attention. In Los Angeles the public-access shows start at noon (I guess they're just too much to view before lunch) and drag on till midnight. In the beginning there was a waiting list to get on public access. But as the idea got old, only the neediest—the ones whose mission was so urgent—stuck around while the thrill seekers dropped out. And many of the traditionally fringy elements of the gay community, eager to make up for years of invisibility or negativity, have clamped on to public access like lampreys. Who can blame them? The need to validate one's existence by being seen on TV (Buck Henry wrote in his screenplay for *To Die For,* "You're nothing if you're not on TV") is the new American neurosis.

So you can watch a show in which a man pretends to be Barbra Streisand for half an hour, lounging with a cup of tea and making phony phone calls to the outside world. Or you can enjoy a drag queen minister who looks like the illegitimate spawn of Ethel Merman and Marjorie Main, preaching love from, I think, Sacramento. There are endless panels on living with AIDS, and these are very good. There are also lots of shows where self-appointed reporters lug their camcorders to gay pride festivals and broadcast all those images we've been asking the straight media not to show. The Right invariably seizes on these—they have little else left, really—but the price of a free and out society is allowing ourselves to be seen, warts and all. Right, Left—we're all getting our kicks on Channel 66.

# Let's Take Over P-Town

If you haven't been to Provincetown, Mass., and you call yourself a homosexual (or others call you one), you really owe yourself a trip. It's the closest thing we have to a theme park, though I'm not exactly sure what the theme is.

Earlier this summer I was in Peetown (that's the logo they put on the souvenir diapers—I'm not kidding; straight tourists buy them) watching the British turn Hong Kong over to the

Chinese. There was bonny Prince Charlie, expressing his deep affection for the colony his mother was about to lose. He was handing Hong Kong back to the people who, after all, really make the town tick. And all I could think was, *When are they going to turn Provincetown over to the people who make it tick?*

Provincetown's been gay at least since I was a child, when we were told not to bother the artists, which was code for *stay away from any men wearing Capri pants and a scarf.* The main drag (and there's plenty of it) is called Commercial Street, although in the old days it wasn't quite so commercial. It was quaint, which was code for *run-down.* Now, of course, the art galleries rub elbows with the key-chain shops and the straight tourists gape openly at the parade of tattooed, hand-holding, ass-grabbing, platform-heel-wearing gay tourists.

Naturally, we are up to the challenge. There are moments walking down Commerical Street when you feel like you're in Disneyland, wearing the Goofy costume. Just being there and looking however you want to look, you're part of the entertainment. Some of us like to play for the crowd, some of us would rather they didn't stare, and some of us just want them to go away as much as they want us to.

The town makes a big deal out of the diversity and mutual tolerance of its residents, but that tolerance turns out to have severe limits. Bars close at 1 A.M., just when things are getting going, and hundreds of *descamisados*—shirtless ones—empty into an area of Commercial Street in front of a pizza parlor. It's eerie to watch the nightly ritual. A few dozen gather first, perched on the steps like the birds waiting for Tippi Hedren. Then the bigger bars shutter, and it's Times Square on New Year's Eve, only everybody's polite. A tall blond drag queen on a motorized skateboard zips in and out of the crowd dispensing cheer. Lesbian couples, noticeable chiefly because they keep their shirts on, mingle with the gay men. Everybody is marking time. It's a long night until the sun comes up and you baste yourself like a Thanksgiving turkey on the chaise lounges of the boat slip.

Slowly a group breaks off and makes its way to the hallowed part of the harbor formerly known as the Dick Dock. This is a pier, under and around which lots of moonlit sexual activity used to take place. The new owners, apparently in collusion with the township, have hired guards and put in lights and more or less put an end to all this.

These days the playground is closed after hours, along with the rest of the town. This curfew costs Provincetown tens of thousands of dollars' worth of business, but, of course, it's only gay business, and the money would be made only by gay businesspeople.

The straight businesspeople who run the tourist shops and sight-seeing trolleys don't stand to make any money late at night. So why should they change the rules? They're in the majority, especially in the winter, when the big decisions are made at town meetings attended only by the hardy year-rounders, descendants of the Portuguese fishermen who claimed their toehold in the New World on this nail of the claw of New England.

These are the same people who tell you that the season is short and they have to grab every dollar they can between Memorial and Labor days. (They'd prefer straight dollars, but they'll *tolerate* ours.) With that in mind, they've joined us in an uneasy truce, much as we've seen between the Chinese and the British in Hong Kong.

In a flip side to Hong Kong's tale, I think the people who originally colonized P-town should turn it over to the people who have recolonized it: us. You think we can't make this happen? Of course we can. We'd just have to move the elections to August—when you can open any door in town and hear a Bette Davis impression.

**That Old Sinking Feeling**

There were no gay people on the *Titanic*. I've seen a dozen movies, a musical, an opera, a Vegas tableau—everything but a dog-show version—and short of a few guys putting on dresses to sneak their way into the lifeboats, I've yet to find a hint of anything interesting going down but the *Titanic* herself. Even the Nazis, who made a gigantic melodrama designed to show how the British class system and rich Jews conspired to sink the ship, neglected to include us in their take.

Maybe this is the real reason the *Titanic* story clanks loudly through the corridors of time. It's a haven for people who are afraid to confront The Gay Angle in popular culture. You can dip into a *Titanic* story secure in the knowledge that Colonel Astor was not traveling with a "nephew" named Zack, Mr. and Mrs. Strauss had not been married in Hawaii, and the unsinkable Molly Brown was not a diver.

This plays large with the legion of people lately who whine, "Must everything be so gay?" as if millions of gay people just showed up last week on some alien craft. In a way, of course, it's true: In the past year millions of formerly invisible gay people came out. The reliable right demonized us, but the slurs seemed increasingly hollow to a straight public presented with our everyday gayness. It's all right to be gay, this public seems to be saying. Just don't be so pushy about it.

Be happy that a major television network lets you tell comic lesbian love stories. But don't fuss when that network puts an "advisory" in front of the show. Be grateful when religious or governmental institutions tell you it's OK to be gay so long as you don't actually engage in any homosexual behavior. At least they don't hate you anymore right out of the box.

Understand that when corporations refuse to support expressions of gay culture, it's nothing personal. They simply wish to avoid controversy. Know that when ex-Secretary of Education William Bennett throws around pseudodata claiming that the life expectancy of an American gay male is forty-three years, he's not a hatemonger; he just wants the gay community to clean up its act. In fact, remember that anyone who goes on Bill Maher's TV show and offers the opinion that sex causes AIDS isn't being mean-spirited, just a little confused in her terminology. In other words, there was a small problem with some ice, we'll be slightly delayed getting to New York, and in any event, there's enough room in the lifeboats for everybody.

Your straight friends—and some of your gay ones—who want you to just pipe down and be a little less gay are wringing out the last vestiges of homophobia injected into them years ago. Many of them don't know they have it. When Frank Oz, director of *In & Out,* tells the media that the movie's restricted rating is important because the picture isn't for children, that's not Frank Oz the gay-friendly artist talking. It's Frank Oz, product of a generation that believes homosexuality and young people don't mix. When Tony Danza zaps Ellen and Anne for displaying affection in front of the president, that's not the Tony Danza who helped his young costar Danny Pintauro come to terms with his sexuality. It's Tony Danza the street fighter hanging on to the last shred of prejudice Brooklyn gave him. When Tom Selleck sues a tabloid because its claims about him are false and his family is hurt to read such falsehoods (none of the other falsehoods hurt?), this is not the Tom Selleck who deals with gay people every day of his life but a guy from a generation that was told that gay equals bad.

What we must realize is that homophobia is the status quo, so insidious and ingrained that it will sneak up on us in the most unexpected and casual places. Most people don't question the status quo, especially people who are not by nature revolutionaries. Certainly the 1,500 people who died on the *Titanic* didn't do a lot of questioning. The men put the women in lifeboats and stayed behind. The steerage passengers allowed the crew to lock them away while the first-class passengers made their escape. People followed custom—all the way to the bottom of the Atlantic. Who would have guessed that, as far back as that cold April night in 1912, silence equaled death?

# As Gay As It Gets

I was watching the Super Bowl with Lea DeLaria, the stand-up comic who could be mistaken for Lou Costello. Lea's famous for opening her act by racing across the stage and bellowing at the top of her lungs, "Good evening! I'm a b-i-i-ig dyke!" In a roomful of gay boys pretending to watch the Super Bowl—which is, let's face it, the Academy Awards for straight people—DeLaria was the only one actually following the game.

Not only following it but capable of explaining it to the puzzled faces around her. The rest of the group looked at the set only when Martha Reeves and the Vandellas came out to sing during the "Tribute to Motown" halftime show (and it's probably time for Smokey Robinson to stop singing "Take a good look at my face," at least in close-ups on TV if you know what I'm saying).

So Lea was lecturing a group of highly educated professionals on the finer points of first downs, onside kicks, and tight ends, the last of which actually got their attention for a minute. You know, we all hate to see stereotypes being reinforced, but when you're part of a group of Hollywood gay boys listening to a pretty butch lesbian tell you about football, you're not only reinforcing a stereotype, you're living one. Sometimes, in spite of our best efforts to mainstream ourselves and prove we're as Normal As Anyone, we suffer a tiny lapse.

The networks must have suspected this would happen. On CBS they countered the game with a rerun of the Bette Midler *Gypsy*. PBS had an evening of Kander and Ebb and Julie Andrews, and Comedy Central ran an *Absolutely Fabulous* marathon. Even the old-movie stations, which run tons of Westerns, war movies, and gangster pictures, were running daylong blocks of musicals. Think their marketing people all read the same memo?

I was thinking about—let's not call it stereotypical—conventional gay behavior during one of the breaks in the Super

Bowl telecast (that would be when the teams were playing) when someone mentioned how good he thought Greg Kinnear was in the James Brooks comedy *As Good As It Gets*. If you haven't seen it, he plays a successful New York painter with a swell apartment who, when he gets beaten up, seems to have no health insurance, no sales, no friends, and nowhere to live. Oh, yes, and he's gay—primarily, as far as I could tell, so he can serve as a nonsexual plot device later on to help the straight hero and heroine get together.

Don't get me wrong. Kinnear is very good in this movie, and he was a good shot at winning the Oscar. But I wonder what about his performance makes him gay. Other than the script's telling us, repeatedly, that he's gay, when does he have a moment of overt homosexuality? Is there intimacy with a man? Is there even anything stereotypical, other than a cuddly dog and an even more ambiguous manager, played with strategic jewelry by Cuba Gooding Jr.? Do shy smiles and a certain softness make a nonentity gay? (Of course, compared with Jack Nicholson, DeLaria is soft.) In the absence of a fully realized character—and for all the big scenes they've given him, I don't think he has one here—Kinnear shows admirable restraint in not falling into a stereotype to make his point. Maybe that's what my friend meant.

In *My Best Friend's Wedding*, Rupert Everett, who was overlooked by the Academy, is allowed to exhibit all the showy, big-city gay mores because he's passed off as a straight man pretending to be gay when he is really a dyed-in-the-vicuña queen. So he gets to be a gay man making fun of gay stereotypes. Sophisticated and elegant in his real life, he exaggerates his mannerisms to convince straight people—who, presumably, otherwise wouldn't know—that he's gay. This is a funny comment and, to my mind, much more believable than what Kinnear is asked to play.

Everett's flirting with Julia Roberts seems real, as if he could possibly take a plunge with her. Kinnear's flirtation with Helen Hunt is pure plot contrivance. The Everett character is a whole person, not just a gay person. Ultimately that's what will happen in movies and TV as gay characters move to the next level. Gay life, as lived at Super Bowl parties, will just have to catch up.

**Blowing in the wind**

"I'm so glad to be in New York at the Gay Men's Health Crisis instead of in Washington at the Straight Men's Health Crisis." This got a huge laugh when Bette Midler said it a few weeks ago at a benefit for the GMHC. Here was an audience that for almost fifteen years has been hearing how promiscuity is a big homosexual problem. All of a sudden the other nine guys in the random sample are having to worry about it—and at the highest level of government. Sex panic, indeed.

True, they're worrying for different reasons, but at least we have temporarily relinquished possession of the scarlet letter. Monica S. Lewinsky, as the *New York Times* amusingly refers to her each and every time (just in case you get her confused with Monica J. Lewinsky or Monica Q. Lewinsky), has been Monica from heaven for comedy writers. Now we know the identity of Deep Throat. The new national bird is the spread eagle. Monica's dry-cleaning problems give new meaning to the term *Whitewater*. You've heard 'em. I got paid for some of 'em.

Sexual malfeasance among the governing elite has always been a surefire cash cow for the comedy business. At the same time, Xena's double-edged sword of political correctness has transformed old-fashioned sexual carryings-on into newfangled sexual harassment. The feminist movement almost drained all the humor out of sex (out of life itself there for a few years). Whether you liked her or not, Anita Hill isn't funny. You knew she represented what was really going on in companies all across America.

But we haven't seen many feminists springing to Lewinsky's defense. It took Kathleen Willey, who charges a man with sexual harassment and then writes him fan letters, to get them into action. I think Monica's poor showing had to do with a lot of people of the boomer generation having enough life experience to realize that (a) everybody lies, (b) it takes two to tango or even to do the horizontal bop, and (c) in a world where truth is so shadowy, performance and the bottom line are what count.

Studies taken before Willey's toxic spill on *60 Minutes*, during the early weeks of the Lewinsky hostage crisis (poor thing couldn't leave her apartment; even Madonna gets to go to the park and jog!), indicated over and over that the American public, sometimes by a 75 percent majority, thought the media were making too much of the thing. Clinton's approval ratings climbed even after the Annan-Hussein agreement doused all hopes of a big, butch war. And a CNN poll revealed that only 12 percent to 16 percent of Americans think the president is obliged to set a moral standard. At the millennium Americans view their leader not as a rabbi or a big Boy Scout but as a CEO. No office sex scandal is going to get a CEO fired when the stock is up. Most Americans want to keep the president's personal moral standards separate from his politically moral ones. Feminists certainly do. Especially when the president is pro-choice.

Do gay people? Does anyone find it ironic that a president who stated that gay marriage is unalterably wrong is now embroiled in a scandal involving alleged adultery in a straight marriage? Some Clinton spin doctors attempted to separate adultery from oral sex. Is eating cheating? Talk about splitting hairs. Maybe the administration's new motto should be "Do as I say, not as I do. And while you're at it, do me."

Naturally, it wouldn't be a real sex scandal unless some of the sex was what used to be called *unnatural*. One theory floating around claimed that Bill was up to what he was up to because Hillary is a lesbian. How come nobody ever used this rationale on Jackie Kennedy when her husband was out combing Georgetown for a bite? Well, even the Republicans liked Jackie. She conquered France.

If you don't like a woman, if she doesn't respond to your entreaties, she must be a lesbian. It's literally the oldest argument in the world. Hillary's spent a lot of time ignoring powerful men, so it's her turn in the barrel. But the spin didn't really stick with that one, so it went away.

Being gay is not entirely the stigma it used to be. Even Strom Thurmond, that hoary old bigot, offered the opinion that the only way Clinton could be drummed out of office now was if he were found in the sack with a young boy. Not a man, you'll notice. Not even a boy. A *young* boy. Even Strom Thurmond is beginning to notice something different blowing in the wind.

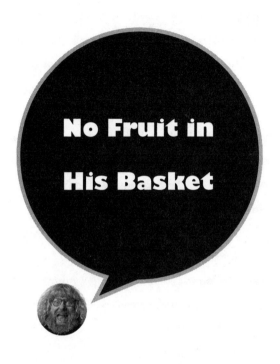

# No Fruit in His Basket

It is as bad to pose as a thing as to be the thing itself, according to the marquess of Queensberry, the man who, ironically, invented the concept of not hitting below the belt, in his 1895 attack on Oscar Wilde. The marquess was covering his losses. If by some chance he couldn't prove that Oscar was a "somdomite" (his own spelling)—and thereby get at Wilde legally—he could at least wound him socially by accusing him of posing as one. To pose as a homosexual was scandalous enough. Back then. In the Victorian age.

Of course, hairs that fine are rarely split today. You're in, or you're out. There is a major tabloid industry that does nothing but track rumors, but rumors about sexuality are roped in with rumors about conspiracy, alcoholism, drug addiction, family tragedy, and UFO abductions. Rumors about people's sexuality are so common, and so many publicly out people lead so many mainstream sorts of lives, that you wouldn't suppose a mere rumor could be enough to bother anyone.

My E-mail box is so crammed with rumors that there is hardly room for the free teen-sex videos; or the get-rich-quick-using-only-baking-soda-and-your-own-belly-button-lint scheme; or the chain letter that was broken only once, by the unfortunate Fatty Arbuckle (and look what happened to him!); or the chance to gamble online with someone in Egypt; or the heartfelt plea, forwarded many times over, to help Little Jimmy find a good lung. With all the juicy rumors going around, I can't find a clear path for the spam.

So it's always bracing when somebody thinks his or her rumor has somehow gotten through the service-for-forty-eight dish and actually had an impact. What's even more amazing is when there is no rumor but someone decides there might someday be one and the time to take action is now, just in case! Sort of like the old days, when they would marry a gay star off before he was big enough for rumors to start. That is the affliction that apparently has struck poor old Milton Berle.

Uncle Miltie, now ninety-one and still a ferocious presence in the Friars Club card room, has been appearing in drag for as long as I can remember. Sometimes he's Carmen Miranda, a huge fruit basket perched precariously on his head. Sometimes he's a face-lifted Florida matron with lipstick on his teeth. He's been doing this since the early '50s. He's also been married many times since then, has written of a torrid affair he claims to have had with Marilyn Monroe, and has gotten untold mileage off the untold mileage of his member, reputed to be the largest in Hollywood history, with the possible exception of Trigger.

Now along comes a big-bucks real estate company designed to show the diversity of its clientele. They run a photo of Miltie as Miranda and an ad line about every queen needing a castle. Milton promptly puts down his cigar and calls his lawyer.

This guy's explanation of why The Divine Uncle M is suing is fairly hilarious, if it weren't so tragic: A younger generation, unschooled in the legend and love of Milton Berle, might be led by this ad to believe that he is gay.

Berle's court complaint, prettied up in PC-speak, makes a show of saying he "respects the rights of others in the pursuit of their own individual sexual orientation." Sure. Whatever.

Obviously in his eyes it's wrong to be gay or even to be seen as gay—$6 million worth of wrong.

Naturally, even a rank homophobe would have to admit that the younger generation referred to in the suit probably would not even recognize Milton in a suit. And second, as we careen into the new millennium, what makes someone who has been in show business all his life and has been notoriously heterosexual for all his ninety-one years think that being mistaken for a gay man could be anything more than a silly joke? After all our wailing and hand-wringing and positive action, could it be that one hundred years has meant nothing?

The Milton of Queensberry is back, and posing as a thing is once again as bad as being the thing itself. Remember that the next time someone like me tells you things are getting better. It's just a rumor.

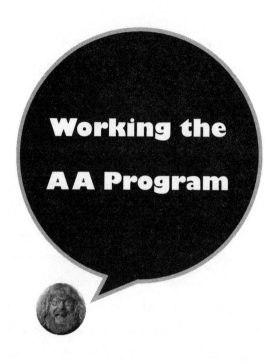

# Working the AA Program

It's Oscar time again, which means you're going to start reading lots of columns that begin with that sentence—including this one. If you're still with me, it means you have a generally healthy homosexual interest in (a) movies, (b) movie stars, (c) gorgeous women in ugly dresses, (d) hunks in tuxedos, and (e) earnest lesbian documentarians with political agendas and ugly dresses. For hunks in ugly dresses, you'll have to wait for the Tonys.

For the past six years, I have been part of the team of writers that comes up with much of what you hear coming out of the mouths of those babes. The first show I actually shared credit for was the infamous Snow White year—although I honestly did not come up with (or write) that particular number. In truth, if you are an Oscar buff, you know in your deepest heart of darkness that it was no worse than Teri Garr dancing on an airplane wing while singing "Flying Down to Rio." Only Rio didn't sue. Snow White had more hype, and she also had Rob Lowe, who had the misfortune of performing a much more scandalous number on another videotape that was unearthed two weeks later. Because of the brouhaha with Disney, the Academy has deleted the piece from its official tapes of the show. I keep hoping they'll put the other Rob Lowe number on instead.

In the years I have been doing the show, we have also been gifted with sea horses and crabs singing tunes from *The Little Mermaid,* Placido Domingo doing the mambo, and a bunch of chorus boys in buffalo skins slouching around a fake campfire to the strains of the theme from *Dances with Wolves.* It makes me feel like the whole world owes Allan Carr a box of chocolates.

Since the no-host Snow show, the proceedings have been reined by Billy or Whoopi. (If we could get Robin to join in, we could do Oscar Relief.) They are both total delights, and this year when they both found other things to do with themselves, I thought I would get to revert to my old Oscar Chinese food, laughing and pointing and flinging the occasional egg roll at the screen. (Jack Valenti was a favorite target.)

Like a true AA follower (as in Academy Awards, not 12 steps), I never cared for Oscar parties. Somebody always talked through the songs or Vanessa Redgrave's speech or the costume parade, in which elegant runway models were forced to dress up as the farmers in *Places in the Heart.* There was always a pool, and it was always won by some bimbo who hadn't been to the movies all year but picked all the winners that had the same names as her dead cats. Somebody always asked—loudly and more than once—what the hell art direction was and why the British pictures weren't eligible for the foreign-language film award.

So I would stay in my West Hollywood apartment, which was just as well, because Oscar night is a national holiday in the Creative City. Absolutely *everybody* tunes in, and out here that means silence reigns from about 4:30 P.M., which is when the local stations (and now E!) begin broadcasting the equivalent of the pregame show. It's a ninety-minute orgy of limousine disgorgements and Alec Baldwin and Kim Basinger bravely facing broad daylight and high winds to stand on a platform and chat with Army Archerd, the razor-sharp columnist who is the only conscious link between the new Hollywood and the old.

If Army ever retires, it will be to the Smithsonian. At 6 o'clock the actual show starts, still in broad daylight. And for the next few hours—if you keep your windows open—you will hear ricocheting from canyon to canyon shrill exclamations such as "Ohmigod, is that Demi Moore? What has she got *on?*" At about 7:30 the pizza-delivery boy arrives: "Domino's. Got your pizza. Did you see Demi Moore? What did she have *on?*"

I won't be indulging in this ritual this year. I have once again been asked to work, this time with David Letterman. It's going to be an interesting year. Not only is Dave based in New York, but he is really not a Hollywood player. Billy and Whoopi and everybody else who has hosted the show are movie stars. Even Johnny Carson, when he was hosting, was based in Burbank and widely conceded to be as much of a star as anyone else in town and as much of an inside industry force. Letterman is a true maverick as far as the movies are concerned. The fear is that he won't really be at the party—he'll be standing outside on the deck making fun of the party. I think he's too smart for that. I also think he has broadened his base—if that isn't too Oprah an analogy—and has a real love of movies and the idea of movie stars. But he *is* Dave. As they say at Forest Lawn: Remains to be seen.

As for this year's crop of gay protests, rape is not sex, and those who can't differentiate probably shouldn't see *Pulp Fiction* or any other movie beyond *The Lion King*. And if you really think that Scar in *The Lion King* is a gay stereotype, you need to spend a few weeks in London or snuggled in with the films of Laurence Olivier or Jeremy Irons or Alec Guinness.

This is also the year of *Four Weddings and a Funeral,* with its truly noble depiction of a gay couple facing life, death, and straight people. It's nominated for Best Picture, and its hunk star will be there in a tuxedo. So break out the kung pao chicken and enjoy the carnival.

# About the Author

Bruce Vilanch, whose monthly column "Notes from a Blond" appears in *The Advocate,* lives in Los Angeles and can be seen nightly on *Hollywood Squares* and backstage at most every other Hollywood function and dysfunction.